RUNNING WITH
HORSES

Praise for

WE WERE

WOLVES

'A truly original and affecting piece of work'
Phil Earle

'This beautiful, tensely written book is a classic of its kind . . .
beautifully written, taut and tense'
Melvin Burgess

'Yearning regret punctuated by glimpses of real companionship
and pure dread. What a joy to see Jason's pictures matched by
such an unsentimental but tender story'
Geraldine McCaughrean

'Wild and unsettling and extraordinary'
Maggie Harcourt

'This powerful, unsentimental novel calls to mind the work of
Patrick Ness and David Almond, and their capacity to be both
topical and timeless'
Irish Times

'A beautifully-written atmospherically illustrated *tour de force*'
LoveReading

RUNNING WITH
HORSES

Written and illustrated by
JASON COCKCROFT

ANDERSEN PRESS

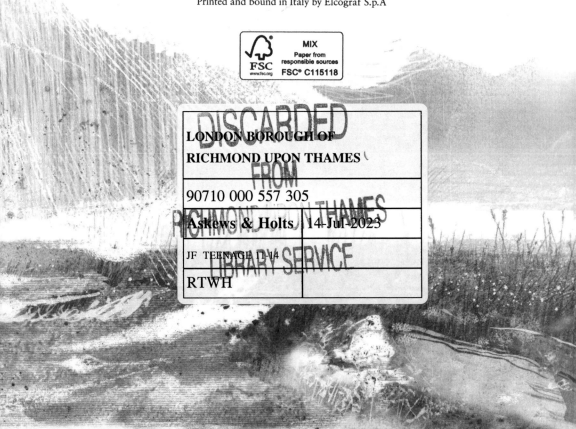

This edition first published in 2023 by
Andersen Press Limited
20 Vauxhall Bridge Road, London SW1V 2SA, UK
Vijverlaan 48, 3062 HL Rotterdam, Nederland
www.andersenpress.co.uk
2 4 6 8 10 9 7 5 3 1

First published in hardback in 2022 by Andersen Press Limited

British Library Cataloguing in Publication Data available.

ISBN 978 1 83913 314 5

Printed and bound in Italy by Elcograf S.p.A

*For the loved ones in my life,
and for those that are absent.*

I was angry with my friend;
I told my wrath, my wrath did end.
I was angry with my foe:
I told it not, my wrath did grow.

A Poison Tree, William Blake

I thought the dreams were over and all in the past, and then the horse came.

A white horse it was, and beautiful. Eye as shiny as a marble, and teeth long like piano keys, candle-white. It came one night in my dreams, its breath hot and the sudden splash of moonlight on the mane bright enough to blind me.

I'd had dreams like it before, but this one was different. Because the horse wasn't a beast or a monster like in the past, nothing ancient and fearful. Just a horse. And I wasn't afraid when I saw it. At least, not for myself, because this great beautiful creature was running from something I couldn't see. Something that was hidden deep in the clouds on the horizon, in the waves.

Something that meant the horse harm.

Arriving soon, and never to settle.

PART ONE

ONE

CALL ME RABBIT.

It's not my name. Not my proper name.

My mam and dad would never have called me such a barmy thing, even as a joke. But Rabbit is what Joe called me, because for a while I didn't talk. First day me and Mam turned up at the caravan park, Joe clapped eyes on me and he laughed himself silly and said I was quiet as a rabbit. And the name stuck, just like that.

When I say I didn't talk, I mean it. I wasn't in a sulk, and I wasn't having a bad day, neither. And I wasn't taking it out on anyone, if that's what you think. I just didn't talk, not at all, not a word, and for months. And not just with Joe, but everybody.

At the time, most folk thought I had a speech impediment, something wrong with my voice box or something, but that's not what it was. Thing is, I never was much of a talker anyway, but they weren't to know that. My dad used to say, 'There are those that Talk and those that Do, and be bloody glad you're not one of the first lot.'

Although, if he'd talked more about the things that bothered him, I'm thinking maybe he'd still be alive. Maybe he wouldn't have ended up dead in the woods, because that's what happened. And maybe I wouldn't have had to watch him die. Maybe things would have been different and I wouldn't have stopped talking, because that's what was behind it – me seeing something no lad should ever have to see.

This story isn't about my dad, though, it's about Joe and me and that summer we found the bloke down the hole. But before I get to that, there was something else he said, my dad, something he'd read somewhere. He said that there are two sorts of truth. There's the truth that Lights the Way, and there's the truth that Warms the Heart. Well, if you ask me there's a third sort – the truth that you have to get out no matter what. That's the truth I'm going to tell, because it's the only one I know.

And my truth starts and ends with Joe Fludde's smile.

I could draw you his teeth right now – straight and white and the one chipped dogtooth on the right that snagged on his top lip when he talked and gave him this baby-faced look that seemed to make a nonsense of all the stories about him. Like how he was a thief from a family of thieves, for instance, and a liar and vandal, too. Then there were the rumours of the fires, because the fires were all folk talked about that summer: the farm fires and who'd set them, and whose place would burn down next. And you can guess who they thought was behind it all. There'd been half a dozen that we knew about – barns and outhouses and store sheds and that. It had been going on for months now, and the police were everywhere you turned, searching out the culprit, and not having much luck with it, either.

This was in East Ferry, where me and Mam had moved to, which is somewhere you won't have heard of, probably. Nice town by the sea, quiet in winter and overrun with tourists in summer. But like any little town, it has its odd ways, and if you'd bothered listening to them, folk here would have told you that the fires hadn't been set by anyone born in East Ferry. Because anyone barmy enough to have burned people's property couldn't be from around here, had been their logic. See, the arsonist must have been an outsider, and there was no bigger outsider than Joe and his family – no matter that they'd lived there most of Joe's life. But that's how it was – if you weren't born in East Ferry, then you were an incomer, and shame on you if you thought different.

It wasn't a bad place, though, if you ignored the daft talk. In fact, I liked it. I liked the slow pace of things on the coast, and the quiet. Liked the sea air and the fields and the wild of it all.

It was dead different than the town where I came from, and there were things I missed about my old life, of course. I missed Mam's house back on the estate in our town, for starters. I missed the nearby canal, and the stream and the woods leading out to the fields, where I used to walk and watch the fish and birds. And there were other things I missed, too – things that were gone for ever, never to come back. Like Dad.

But see, in my old town you never got to watch seals lazing on a beach, and you never dug fossils out of the cliffs with your bare hands, either. So, all in all, I thought it was just fine out here.

Joe, though, he didn't have any time for East Ferry. He said the place was cursed.

'You and me will always be aliens here, Rabbit,' he told me the day it started. 'Mark my words.' It was the first Sunday of the holidays, and we were running across the cliff, dashing against the blue sky heavy with insects and gulls, and Joe, he looked over and gave me a grin. 'Aliens, I tell you – *like that David Bowie bloke, except without the funny eyes.*'

Bowie was one of our things – me and Joe. He was a dead rock star from the seventies who dressed up like he was from outer space, and he had two different-coloured eyes. God's honest truth. Proper outsider, he was. We both liked him, me because Dad had always played his records when he was home from the army, and Joe, on account his old man was in a tribute band once, he says. Not that he had many memories of his dad, apparently, because he scarpered when Joe was still a nipper.

Anyway, it was Joe's catchphrase: *Like that David Bowie bloke, except without the funny eyes.*

He said it nearly every week, as though it was the first time I'd heard the joke. And always that smile of his, bright as daytime lightning. Most beautiful smile you've ever seen, and I'm not even joking.

So there we were, me and Joe, laughing out loud and running so fast we might take off. And then, as though it was the most natural thing in the world, Joe stops and grabs me by the shoulders and says: 'Here, Rabbit – you wanna see a dead horse?'

TWO

SOMETHING YOU NEED to know about me: I'm not one for trekking all day to see dead things, usually. So you'll be wondering what made me do it then. But you don't know Joe Fludde. See, when Joe smiled at you like that, you didn't say no. Something in him sort of shone out like nothing I'd known before. Like an energy. Something cosmic. Not that everyone felt like me, because they didn't. He had his enemies, all right. But I wasn't one of them, that's all I'm saying.

There's something else you need to know about me, and I might as well get it over with: I used to see things. This was before Joe and the caravan park and the fires. They weren't hallucinations, not really. I'd dream them first off, and then somehow they'd appear to me when I was awake. It was ancient animals I saw – wolves and bears and the like – out in the woods, out with Dad, before he died. Which I know sounds barmy, but he was a Troubled Soul, was Dad. That's what they call him now he's not here any more – a Troubled Soul – although when he was alive they had other names for him, of course. Which is one of the reasons I have no problem with outsiders like Joe. Because Dad was one, and I am, too.

Anyway, these animals – beautiful, they were. Except, you see, they weren't there, they couldn't have been. I'd made them up, or we had. Him and me.

It's not something you can easily tell people, though. As soon as anyone hears that you've been seeing stuff, you get a bad reputation real quick – and then, just like that, you're a mental case.

Course, they don't call you that. They're too polite. Louise, my counsellor, she says there are lots of common mental conditions, and it's lucky that I wasn't the type that sat in bed all day waiting for the world to end, or lined up the cutlery on the table, just so, because I thought it would protect my family from car accidents or plane crashes or fatal diseases.

Which is true, all right. But I was the sort instead that dreamed up ancient creatures out of the ground, which I'm not sure is any better. And, yeah, it might sound funny when you try to picture it, like it's some cartoon, but I can tell you it wasn't funny when it happened to me.

Dad was a bit of a dreamer. He said the world was full of ancient animals and magic, and we were just passing by. He meant people. He had a way of talking that made things come alive – a bit like Joe – and when he spoke of nature and history it was as though I could see it in my dreams, all the creatures of the forests, every animal that had ever lived. Like they'd passed from his mind into mine. That's how close we were, me and him. Maybe some of the madness passed from him to me, too, I'm thinking.

Anyway, the dreams of wolves stopped pretty quick about a year ago, the same time the night sweats kicked in, and the shaking, the Scares. And that's when I first stopped talking.

Not long after my dad got killed.

I was there when it happened, saw it all go down. This is the story, if you want to know: he'd got into trouble with some bad men, gangsters. Not that he was bad, because he wasn't. But he'd had a tough life, and Louise says sometimes that no matter how strong or good a man is, life can become overwhelming, and that leads to bad decisions being made. And Dad, well, he made a bad decision, and ended up getting shot in the woods, which is something no one deserves, especially him. And me, I watched it happen, like I say.

Then came the Scares.

That's what I call them: the Scares. Because they come up on me like a horror film – some feeling that a terrible thing is gonna happen. And I'll be proper frightened, shaking with the fear. Like the worst panic attack you've ever had, but nothing is wrong, see.

No reason for it. Not as far as you can tell, anyway.

Louise says it's the wiring in my brain telling me I'm in danger, because in the past there *had* been danger. On that day in the woods. It's like a stuck record, she says. My primitive mind playing that same danger over and over, and reacting to it. Running scared, like a rabbit.

She means my dad and what happened to him. But she never mentions it right off, just lets me make my own way to the Meaning of it All. Death and Grief and all that. This is how they talk, counsellors, and always the same calm, quiet voice that makes you feel like you're going a bit deaf.

If you look at it, it's remarkable, she tells me. This is Louise again.

That's the word she uses – *remarkable*. Meaning amazing, meaning good. Meaning I'm not a complete basket case. Because when there *was* danger, that mind of mine knew exactly what to do – to run like stink, away from whatever was after me. She calls it my lizard brain. But me, I call it my rabbit brain. It's right down at the base of the skull, she says, the old part that goes back to when we were all walking around naked and hunting bears and living in caves. Times my dad would have loved, probably, because he liked the woods and hunting and foraging, and he was good at it. And when I dream about him – and I do, more times than I'd ever admit to Louise – well, it's always him and me in the woods, tracking pheasant or rabbit or something.

Anyway, what Louise tells me is this: it's got one function. She's talking about my rabbit brain again. All it has to do is get scared and do something about it. Most people freeze, some run. I seem to sweat a lot and kick about in my bed so hard that I can't sleep in it any more, which seems like a pretty useless rabbit brain to me. Because when you wake up crying and your sheets are soaked through, then it's hard to pat yourself on the back for being a remarkably evolved creature, isn't it?

But Louise, she tells me not to look at it like that.

She says I'm a Work in Progress.

She says I'm a Survivor.

She says I'm Doing Just Fine.

And something she did must have worked, because after a while I began talking again. Not that I've ever been a loudmouth, but at least now I don't feel like I'm choking when I open my gob. And the Scares started to come less often, too. Now I only have to see Louise once every couple of weeks, which seems more than enough.

Thing is, right from the start she didn't mind that sometimes I didn't say anything. If I sat there for forty-five minutes saying bugger all, she'd just sit it out with me, like it was a silent staring competition. She didn't take it personally. I liked her for that.

It's why I liked Joe, too.

THREE

Anyway, here we are, me and Joe, and it's the hottest summer on record and we're yomping through the hogweed and nettles, and it's a proper beautiful morning. Blue sky and not a bit of wind. And it's baking on your back, hot as an oven making your skin prickle, so you feel alive, and for once it's like I'm a kid instead of an old man with night sweats and a dead dad haunting his dreams.

We're on our way to the horse Joe was talking about.

'Big lovely nag. You'll see, Rabbit. She's beautiful.' And the way he says it, it could be something alive he's talking about, something that might just trot over to us and eat hay out of our hands, instead of something dead. 'Proper thoroughbred, she is, real class.'

Joe's face lights up when he says it, like it always does when he has a new idea in his head, which is most days. He says he saw it last night, this horse, but from a distance, so he couldn't get a proper look. But what he saw, he tells me, was like 'marble under the moonlight, pale and glowing.'

I don't ask how come he was out in the middle of nowhere at night, and without me. But I think it. And later there'll be other thoughts, too, like how come he knew this story of his would get me out here with him? Why a dead horse? Why that particular lie?

'Glowing, it was,' he says, 'bright as a ghost.'

That's how Joe talks.

He doesn't bother reading, but he has a way with words, like a poet. Better, even. And I think if he'd only look at one of the books I give him, maybe he'd write one himself someday. Not that I've always been into books, because I haven't. Time was I didn't see the point, either, but Joe's worse. He says he knows things you don't get from books. Says he absorbs it out of the ether, but me, I think he just talks to his nan a lot, and the rest he gets from YouTube.

Joe knows how to navigate without looking at a compass, knows which rocks have fossils in them, knows how to tickle fish out of a stream, and knows where to find spring water, or so he tells me. He knows the names of death spirits and Native American legends and Viking gods. He knows how to read your palm and tell your future.

The only thing he doesn't know is where he comes from.

Joe always says he's half Welsh. Doesn't know which half.

Maybe my legs, he jokes.

His dad buggered off, and he never knew his mam, so he was brought up by his grandma Win in one of the bungalows on the caravan park. Sometimes I think, maybe that's what we have in common, him and me – missing dads.

'You sure about this horse?' I ask him, once we're thrashing through the barley field, midway there. 'I mean, you know it was dead, right?' Something inside me is hoping he's wrong, because I'm not looking forward to seeing some poor dead thing, not at all. Not on a day like this. It's a day when you feel so hot and calm you might melt into the land itself, quick as a rain shower sucked down into the summer soil until you become part of it. You and the earth and the air, all mixed together.

'Course it was,' says Joe, without looking up, and he's sounding annoyed that I'd even doubt him. But I see that his shoulders are hunched when they're usually lithe and open. His smile's vanished. Proper smiler is Joe, but not so much today.

The sun is slamming down on us hard, but in a good way, and you can smell the summer in it, like it's concentrated one hundred per cent undiluted sunshine, feeding right into the pits of your bones.

'What did it do then, this horse? Have a heart attack?'

'How would I know?'

'I'm just asking,' I say.

'What's up, Rabbit?' Joe replies. 'You scared?'

Truth is I'm not scared, not really. Just wary. Joe's one for adventures, and me, I've learned to like the simple life since coming to East Ferry. If it was anyone else I'd have to argue the point, though. But Joe, he's already onto the next thing, that quick mind of his always running when others are slow.

'Here, do you know the heart of a horse is nine times as big as a bloke's heart?'

He tells me it's the size of a football, and I'm nodding along, because I don't know any better, you see. So I'm Happy as Larry, as Mam says.

Why shouldn't I be? I'm with Joe and we're in a field in the middle of nowhere and not a soul around for miles, and that's where I want to be.

Don't get me wrong. It's not that I'm in love with Joe.

It's not that, not really, although there's plenty who make jokes about it and take the mick when they see us together.

But I do love him.

He gets me, see, he knows me. Me and Joe, we're closer than mates. Close as you can get without being brothers. Not that I tell him any of this, of course. There's a lot I don't tell him. Like the new dreams I've been having.

'Here, what's on your list?' This is Joe talking again. It's how he thinks – in short bursts of nonsense that stay in your head and make you think. 'What's on your list, Rabbit?'

'What sort of list?'

'Your bucket list. Things you want to do before you die. You must have one.'

We've found the old drainage ditch now. That's how you get to the horse, Joe tells me – out to the Cullen farm and through the barley field, down into the ditch, past the fallen tree that looks like a sleeping cow, then across the hill into the valley, by the old, rusted tractor and through the nettles.

The afternoon is clammy – this real humid sweat rising up from the grass that makes it hard to breathe. We're maybe half a mile from the farm. Half a mile from the bloke in the ground, too, but I'm not to know that. I'm still thinking about that horse Joe talked about. And my dream. Because this morning I'd woken from a night of dreaming. And the thing – the strange thing – is that what I'd dreamed about was a horse. A big white horse running from something that I couldn't see, splashing through the tide. Same dream I've had for almost a week now. And what are the odds of that, eh?

So I'm thinking of horses and dreams, and how they've come together. On this day of all days.

'Everyone's got a list.' This is Joe talking. 'Me, before I'm seventeen I got three things on mine. Things I wanna do. Number one, See a dead body. Two, Find treasure. Three, Read my name in the papers.' He counts them off on his thumb and fingers, one-two-three, like a magician who's setting up some trick. Magic's in the air this summer.

'And a dead horse counts as a body, does it?' I say.

'Today it does,' Joe says, and there's that smile again.

Some people smile and they look happy, other people – people like my mam, for instance – can't help looking sad when they smile. But when Joe Fludde smiled there was this charge in the air that made the hair stick up on your arms, and your teeth ache. When he smiled at you, you thought anything could happen, and all it would take was for you to stride out into the world with him and see what it had to offer. At least, that's what I thought. But after things went wrong that summer and me and Joe found ourselves in deep trouble, well, my mind would ask what exactly had been hiding behind that smile of his.

Because, you see, I was about to find out that what folk said about him happened to be true.

It wasn't East Ferry that was cursed. It was Joe Fludde and his family.

FOUR

There's something else I miss from my old life, by the way.

Her name's Sophie.

I haven't mentioned her until now, but she was a girl I knew back in my old town. That's another story. We were sort of in love, me and her, but then the Scares came and I stopped talking to her, and the Shame came, too. Because here's the thing, what I haven't said until now is I should have been able to save my dad. That's how I think, see. He needn't have died if I'd been braver, stronger, if I'd done something different. Although Louise doesn't agree. She says, when bad things happen sometimes no one can stop it. That it wasn't my fault. That it's just the Scares talking, because Shame and Scares are the same sometimes. And Shame eats away at you, like the sea eats away at a cliff. It stops you from confiding in folk. Makes you feel weak.

Anyway, Sophie. When you stop talking to someone without ever telling them why, eventually they stop talking to you. Funny, that. So me and Sophie just drifted apart. Then one day Mam tells me there's a job free, managing a caravan park on the coast, and she's going to apply for it, and things will be better out there, you'll see.

Then we're moving, maybe going for a year, maybe longer. It would do me good, shake me out of my mood, she thinks. She hopes. Maybe get me talking again, get me back to my old self. She's told my counsellor, the first one – he was called Jon, and he was all right, but not as good as Louise – and he says he's happy about it.

I wanted to describe all this to Sophie, of course, but those Scares and that Shame stopped me. By now, me and her had stopped texting, even, and it's like we never knew each other, which is weird. Because we were as close as two people could be, almost like me and Joe. Closer. Proper love, it was.

Mam's plan with the caravan park, it didn't sound like much of an idea to me at the time, to be honest. But the thing is, it works. Not straight away, but it works now. After a while I start feeling like myself again, and the Shame goes.

My head says it's because of Louise, but my heart knows it's all down to Joe.

FIVE

Not far now. We're past the fallen tree that looks like a cow, and nearing the top of the hill. Rusted old tractor to the right. Then it's down, down into more grass. Yorkshire fog, it's called, all purple on top and waving, thick as a tide. And I pretend we're dragging ourselves through water, like the field is flooded, all shimmer-bright and sparkling. Kids' thoughts, but that's what we're like today. Running through the grass and giggling like kids. And this is when life's best, I'm thinking. Days like this, with nothing to worry about, no counselling for a couple of weeks and no school, no thoughts of Dad and no dreams of animals underground. Just Joe and the fields and the sky.

Wait now. Stop. There in the distance.

The barn.

It's this long, low ramshackle sort of mess. All rectangles and black tar and broken windows. Rotting rain gutters dragging off the shingles, an old plastic bath set as a cow trough to one corner, and a hazel tree growing through its roof.

'How come you went without me?' I ask now, hiding the childish hurt in my voice. Because lads aren't supposed to get jealous like that, are they? And not about something so daft. But what I mean is last night when he says he saw the horse, how come he didn't take me with him, because he always does. Because me and Joe, ever since I moved into the caravan park, me and him have done everything together. Stuck together like flypaper, Mam says. Like twins. Stuck like trouble.

The day we moved in, even before Mam and me had had time to unlock the door of our little bungalow, it was Joe climbing up into the removals van and grabbing something to carry. And Mam's eyes on him, like if she wasn't careful, he'd nick something. Nick meaning steal, meaning thieve, meaning rob.

Which he might have done if him and me hadn't struck it off so quick, he tells me after, laughing.

The thing with Joe is he's never short of words, and soon enough he's charmed Mam, too. It's his superpower, he tells me. 'If *your* superpower is to listen and hardly say a word, then mine is turning shit into gold.'

He could talk his way out of a house fire, he tells me. Talk his way out of the grave.

Mam sees it, of course. And later that day she shakes her head and tells me, 'That lad talks trouble.'

But I like the sound of the trouble Joe talks. His trouble sounds like poetry to me.

It doesn't matter if sometimes I don't say much, because he can talk enough for the both of us. Only, right now in the field under the sun, he's struggling for a single word. I can see it. His lips are all stopped up.

He shrugs, eyes down. Brown eyes, he has, dark as a doe's eyes.

'The thing is,' he says, 'Billy came back last night.' This is what he tells me, finally, when he does open his mouth. He has this bashful sort of tone to his voice that doesn't suit him. Because Joe's usually brash not bashful. 'He needed me to drive up the bay with him to help lug some bottles into the pickup.'

The bottles are gas, to plumb into the caravans and run the heating, and there are plenty of holiday parks around here, and money you can make if you can get hold of cheap bottles, then half fill them and sell them full price.

Billy is Joe's half-brother, who comes and goes and always brings a bad smell with him when he does. Different as you can get from Joe. So me, I let it go. Because Joe can't say no to Billy, not if he doesn't want a hiding. And Joe's had enough in his time, that's what I'm guessing. You just have to see how Joe is around him. Skittish and scared, which tells a story, I'm thinking. And bruises that go too deep to be accidental.

Billy's a bastard, all right.

It's still out there, by the way: the barn. It hasn't gone anywhere. Sitting beneath the sky, low and leaning, close enough that we can see the silver of the water in the cow bath shimmer.

The place hasn't moved, and neither have we. Thing is, I'm not sure I want to see a dead horse. I do and I don't. If anyone knows things die, it's me, so I'm not squeamish, not really. But I'm asking myself if I'm so desperate to stare at some sad beautiful thing dead in a field anyhow? On a day like this, where I feel drunk-happy and we could just keep walking and walking until it's dark, and laugh and joke and not bother with anything dead.

Maybe Joe's thinking the same, because we're both standing there, not moving, faces slick with sweat and eyes blinded by the sun.

'You sure it was dead?' I ask again.

'Told you, didn't I?' he says, but Joe looks worried, and I'm thinking maybe he's got Billy on his mind. Because fights and robbing is what Billy's good at, and in and out of prison since he was old enough.

Meaning Billy's the trouble that Mam thinks Joe talks.

'Don't you want to go look?' Joe asks, sort of shy. Sweat on his lip now, and his eyelashes flickering long and black. Good-looking, is Joe, but today there's something jumpy in him. 'Thought you liked animals.'

I want to tell him I *do* like animals, but there's a difference between listening to a thrush sing and me gawping at the carcass of some poor old nag rotting away in a field, and it's a difference Joe doesn't seem to get. Or doesn't want to. 'You first,' I say.

'Yellow belly,' Joe replies, but there's no poison in it, just a phrase. If anything, he sounds more nervous than me. I follow him through the field, and he's idling now, grabbing a handful of grass. A long sheaf of Yorkshire fog that he waves about him to keep away the flies. It cuts past my sight, bright as a horse's tail.

SIX

THE GROUND AHEAD slopes down into a sort of hollow. A marshy stink, something rotten. I half expect to find a stagnant stream at the bottom of it, but instead there's just a dirt track, and a thick of nettles. And there, about ten metres away, is a broken-down fence of sun-bleached timber.

'This is it,' he says.

'This is what?'

He nods to the field, and me, I don't know what I'm supposed to be looking at. I'm expecting a horse on its side, white as soap, and there's only a long, wide field of wilting grass, all green and yellow and shining under the sun. And the black barn sort of seethes over to the left, so hot I can feel the heat coming off it, smell the creosote and tar, sharp and tangy as blood.

'What's going on?' I ask, because something's up that I don't know about. Something that makes Joe's head drop. I look around, all frightened-up now, because it's the same way he stands when Billy's on the scene – humble, like a beaten dog. I hate that look, hate the way he holds himself. Hate the way Billy makes him feel.

'Don't be angry, Rabbit,' Joe says, and his face is a picture. Gone ghostly, like he's seen a murder.

I freeze, just like that.

Don't be angry. It's like when people tell you don't be scared, or don't think of a dead white horse. Your mind can't help it. So Joe telling me not to be angry doesn't help much. Although, honestly, anger is the last thing on my mind. What I'm feeling is a sort of dread. My rabbit brain is telling me to run, and now I'm starting to look around, expecting Billy to show his face. Billy, with his camouflage jacket and tattoos on his hands that are all blue and bleeding dye. Union flags and army badges. Not that he's ever been near an army, just prison. Billy, with a snarl in his voice, and his breath that smells of gaol.

'I didn't know what else to do,' Joe says now in that same stuttering way as before. 'I'm sorry, Rabbit.'

'Angry about what?' I say. 'What am I supposed to be angry about, Joe?'

I'm feeling the panic now, right under my ribs. A fluttering at first, like the feet of something padding across my chest. A rat as big as a hare. This scuttle of fear.

Suddenly, there's a noise to my right that makes me jump. Out in the sad-looking hawthorn that's leaning over the fence, so close to the ground you can't see where the trunk begins.

You won't believe how noisy a wren can be when she's warning you off her nest. Smallest bird you can imagine, but a proper noisy bugger on her day. And there's a hum, too. Closer, this. A low, quiet hum that seems to be getting louder. Me, I'm thinking it's my ears going funny.

27

The heat getting to me, making me feel faint, because it's proper hot now, and no air. But a few more metres and I know what it is, the noise.

Flies. Lots of them. Down low in the grass, buzzing away.

I think I see Joe nod to something, to the grass beyond the broken-down fence. And now I see the doors. Just some old double doors – size of wardrobe doors maybe – laid out flat in the grass. Four or five different layers of paint blistered from the sun and peeling back like the dried-up pages of a book, and the wood underneath mouldered and rotten through. They look like they've been there for years, those doors. Sunk down in the soil, and heavy.

Funny how a load of wood lying in a dirty great field can give you the frights. But they do. Because of the way Joe's holding himself, all stiff.

He still hasn't looked me in the eye, not for minutes now.

'Spit it out. Joe, come on.'

'There's a bloke,' he says, so low I can barely hear him above the noise of the flies.

'A what?'

'A bloke,' he says again. 'In the hole.'

'Bollocks.'

He's a joker, is Joe. You need to know that about him. He likes to make you jump every now and then, make you smile. I'm thinking this is another of his bad jokes, but at the same time I know Joe, and even he can't pretend like this.

'Honest,' he says. 'I couldn't tell you before, Rabbit. I couldn't. You wouldn't have come.'

No, he's not lying and this is no joke. This is proper worry on his face. Proper fear.

'Really. Go look.'

Those little feet on my chest are pounding now, and I'm wishing it wasn't so hot, because there's not much air out here in this field, under this sky. Not today.

I can't breathe. My throat tightens.

'Where's the horse?' I ask, still hoping it's all some prank. But my voice is hard and angry, just like Joe said it would be. 'Joe?'

'Just look,' he says. He doesn't move an inch nearer, though. Standing sideways to the doors, like he can't quite face them.

There isn't a hole, I tell myself. But by the way he's stuck there, too scared to look at me, I know he's right. I know if I pull on that rusty iron handle hard enough, underneath there'll be the hole, just like Joe says. I'm thinking something shallow, because there are no mines around here. And there are no wells. No tornado shelters. This isn't Kansas or something. It's East Ferry. Some boring seaside town where the only excitement we get is because of a nutter burning down barns. And even he's stopped for a couple of weeks.

'*Go on, look,*' he says.

'Help us, then,' I say, licking my lips. 'I'm not doing it on my own.' And we're standing by the doors, looking down, the sound of heat and sky and birds and buzzing around us, so loud I can hardly think.

'Grab hold,' I tell him, and it's not like I want to look, because I don't.
But here I am anyhow, doing what Joe says.

    We wrap our fingers around the one good handle and begin to pull.
The thing's even heavier than I thought. Must be ten centimetres
thick, and old wood, heavy wood,
and solid despite the rot.

'Pull,' I say, through my teeth. Our arms slide against each other, wet with sweat, sticky. And the door comes up, and dead air with it. Warm with a vinegar sharpness.

And I'm looking at a hole in the ground, all right, and hoping to God it's not a grave.

Joe leans back quick, like he doesn't want any part of it. Which is rich, I'm thinking, seeing as he's the one that brought me here. This is all because of him, because of his lie, I'm telling myself, and now he wants away. Some joke. Because there is no horse, I get that now, never was probably. Just a hole.

It's not black down there in the dark. The ground's too hot for that. No, it's a sort of brown haze, dusty.

The place is dark and smells nearly as bad as the marsh stink in the hollow, worse than a dead horse. In one corner a bit of sunlight shines in – enough to show this thing's deep. Below it, bright and morbid, I think I see something move. A gleam of something, far down – at least three metres down – the shine of a tin can, maybe, or an old bottle. Then I realise what it is. It's a bloke's glasses looking up at me from the bottom of the hole.

'Shit.'

I drop the door quick sharp, and there's a thud and you'd think with the weight of the thing there'd be a great gust of air or something when it slams down. But the day's too hot and heavy for that. There's just a soft thud, but low, so it resounds in the ground beneath my trainers. Then I'm back in the nettles, long strides trying to get me away, but calm like nothing's wrong. Like it's all some mistake. And Joe's voice coming after me, heavy as a storm . . .

'Rabbit . . . *Rabbit!*'

SEVEN

MY MAM HAS this thing she says. A phrase: *Looking back is the surest way to lose your future.*

She tells me, 'Too many clever men have fallen down holes in the road when they've been busy gawping over their shoulder.'

It's all cryptic, of course. But she's talking about Dad, how he couldn't move forward from things that happened in his past. How he was full of regrets. And of all the stupid things to come into my head while I'm running, it's that. Some saying. And the truth is, maybe if I'd listened to it and not looked back, things would have turned out different that summer. But I stop long enough for Joe to grab hold of me, and instead of wrestling him off, I say, 'You lied, you bastard. You lied!'

'I know, I'm sorry.'

'Is he dead?' Because that's the first thing in my head – that I've just seen a dead man's face. 'Is the bloke dead, Joe?'

'No, I swear!'

We're in the grass, it's waist high, shining with sun, lighting up our faces. The hole isn't far away. If he is alive, if Joe's right, then he can hear us, the bloke, but I'm too afraid to keep my voice down. 'I'm going back to the park,' I say. 'I'll tell Mam.'

'No, you can't,' says Joe, his hand on my wrist, and a pleading in his eyes. 'I don't know what to do, but we can't tell anyone – *please*.' And he's never like this, never fearful – except when Billy's about. Joe's brave as they come.

'What's he doing down there?' I ask, looking back to the doors. 'Did he fall in?'

I know he hasn't fallen, of course. I'm not stupid, even if I do stupid things – like follow Joe out to the middle of nowhere on a wild goose chase after a horse that never was.

I know blokes don't just fall into holes and then pull the door shut over their head, but I'm holding onto the idea for now, because I'm guessing the truth will be worse.

'Joe?'

'They put him in it.'

'Who?'

He shakes his head. 'They'll skin me alive if I tell you,' he says.

I've never seen him like this. I've watched Joe climb up cliffs so high they give me nosebleeds just to look at them. I've seen him fight kids twice his size, and grin after the beating. But I've never seen him so frightened before. He's trembling, his nose running like he's about to cry.

'I can't say who. I just can't.'

He's all short words now, and a desperate sound to his voice. And I know he means Billy. Because who else would it be? Who else would have taken Joe out here?

'You better tell me,' I say. And I'm angry, it's there in my voice, but I can't be angry at Joe for long when he's like this.

'What's going on, Joe?' I ask, a moment later. 'Please, tell us. Was it Billy?'

He nods, finally, groans, like there's a great weight inside him that wants out, too heavy for him to bear. 'Him and his mates. They put him in there. It's about the fires—'

'Fires?'

'The farm fires.'

I can't work out what he's saying, not at first. It's all too much and too quick.

'The arson,' he says. And me, I must be going daft, because I get the wrong end of the stick. I'm thinking, maybe they've caught the fella. The bloke who's been burning the farms. Here he is in the hole, and they've caught him, Billy and his pack of thugs. But if that's the case, why's Joe so afraid? Why can't he look me in the eye?

'What about the fires?' I say, not understanding. 'Talk to me.'

He says nothing, and then, when he does speak, it all comes out in a soft rush.

'It wasn't me, promise – I didn't want to, but Billy, he – he's behind it, the arson – getting money from the farmers, like protection money, he says – and this fella found out and now – I didn't want to do it, Rabbit, I swear, but you know what the bastard's like – and they're gonna kill him, I know they will – you don't know what Billy and his mates are like but they'll kill this bloke—'

I see him sag, like the life's drained out of him, and I just watch, confused. All I hear, all I can absorb, is *they're gonna kill him.* And don't get me wrong, the bloke in the hole looks nothing like my dad. But something in the way he was sitting there, looking up at me but not looking at me, or the lean of his shoulders or something, well, it set my heart rocking hard in my chest. Just for a second.

Dad.

'We've got to get him out,' I say.

'No!'

'We have to!' I'm yelling. It's him that wants to leg it now, and I'm holding onto him. And what you need to know is, Joe's stronger than me, taller and wider, and if he wanted he could clobber me and run off and I could do nothing about it. But somehow I'm keeping him here. 'You said it yourself, Joe – they'll kill him.'

Funny, isn't it? How the world turns upside down sometimes. I'm the one that always runs, it's my nature, and yet here I am holding brave Joe back. 'Seriously, we have to get him out of there,' I say.

The sun catches Joe's face, and I see something in him change. Some of the fear is melting away, turning to a sort of determination, and if only we had another minute I know he'd agree. One more minute and I'm certain we'd pull back those doors and drag that fella out somehow.

And maybe if things had been different, me and Joe would have done, too. But we never had the chance, see.

I don't know if it's him or me that hears the engine first. But we both turn in time to see the pickup on the horizon, and right away we know who it is, and why he's here.

Billy.

EIGHT

Even from this distance, I recognise one of the shapes in the dark of the windscreen.

I know all the ugly angles of him, his head hunched down, thick shoulders. The truck's rolling over the tracks, rocking from side to side. Slow, but close enough that we can hear the music thudding from the stereo inside.

'We have to go,' Joe says. 'Rabbit, come on!'

But given the direction the truck is coming from, I know Billy will see us if we try to make it back up the bank. So I wrestle Joe's hands off me, trying to keep him low to the fence, out of sight. He doesn't get it straight away, and shoves me away, hard. And, for a second, I admit I think about hitting him. And I've never hit Joe, never even thought about it. But that's how scared I am.

Instead I just say, 'In the trees, quick.' And thank God, finally, Joe understands and does what I say.

We're hunkered down in the nettles, down amongst the hawthorn trees, when the pickup arrives in the field. Hard to think that twenty minutes ago me and Joe were on our way and happy as can be, or I was anyway.

Hard to think how things change so quick. How the course of a life can pivot on a single day, because that's what this is. You can bet on it. Things won't be the same again, not after this. Not for anyone.

Especially Joe.

We're trying not to move even though the nettles are stinging our arms all over, burning like someone's thrown boiling water over us. Flies are buzzing around, and the heat from the ground just won't give up. We're wet with sweat, and doing our best not to shake. From the pain. From the fear. Because if they see us, we're done for. Like the poor bugger in the hole.

There's four of them, including Billy. They climb out of the pickup, two in the front, and the others out of the bed of the truck. I recognise a couple, from when they've been hanging around the caravan park. Laughing, all of them. Their faces are pink with the heat, and there's a sort of drunken look to them. Sure enough, the two from the back drag out a half-finished box of beer and drop it onto the grass.

It's Billy I'm watching, though. He comes striding out, moves to the edge of the doors in the ground, and reaches out a foot before slamming his boot down three times, making the doors ring. They're all grinning at some joke I can't hear for the buzzing of flies and the crackle of heat. The tallest of them pulls back one of the doors, and grabs quickly at his nose, laughing, like he can't believe the stink. Like it's some clowning show. And all of them, having a good time.

Then Billy bends over, takes a bottle of beer out of the box on the ground and moves to the hole. 'You thirsty, Max?' he yells, grinning.

Then, before we know it, he's thrown the bottle down into the hole, hard as you like. Proper slammed it down, like tossing a cricket ball at a wicket. We hear it break, but nothing else. No sound from the bloke down there, not even a whimper.

Bastard, I'm thinking.

Then Billy sends another down, an empty one this time. And soon enough his mates have slung four more empties down there, all breaking. And I'm doing my best not to picture what state the bloke must be in, surrounded by all that broken glass. But they're still laughing, Billy and his mates, having a grand old time. And next to me Joe is so still I'm frightened he's going to do something stupid, like start running or throw himself over the fence.

'*Just wait*,' I say, under my breath. But I'm wanting away just as much as him. Every second we stay here feels like sitting in a fire. And it's not just the nettles, either. It's the whole horrible thing.

I can't watch any more. I don't want to. So as soon as Billy and the others turn for the barn, I pull at Joe's wrist, and then we're crabwalking through the nettles, slow as we can. Our arms are blistered and raw, sort of numb with the pain.

I hear one of them pulling open the barn door. The stereo in the pickup is still playing loud, the engine running, but their attention is on the barn, and they're drinking now.

Soon enough, they're going inside, and we're climbing up through the field, but real low, our faces in the dirt. Looking around every now and then to see if they've noticed us.

Joe and me. Climbing and falling, away from the hollow and the barn. Away from the noise of the truck engine, and the bottles breaking. Away from Billy and his sneers. Away from the poor sod in the ground.

When I'm brave enough to put my head up again, I see Joe next to me, his face livid and gleaming with sweat. Eyes pink and wide. By his startled expression, I know I must look as awful as he does.

Past the tree shaped like a sleeping cow, past the drainage ditch. And now we're running, both of us. My rabbit brain is kicking in at last. Up onto the road, and we finally start to breathe. A blue dazzle on the tarmac leads out to the sea in the distance, and my feet are burning, the soles of my trainers feel soft as I walk, like they've half melted. I'm breathing in and out, like Louise tells me. Deep breath in, and a longer one out, because that's how you calm your blood.

And all the time, I know Joe's beside me.

Funny thing is, neither of us speak. After all we've just seen, we can't find the words.

Call it shock. Our arms are red raw. Sting marks on our faces, too. The air about us is on fire, but my legs are cold, my hands. Shivering. Like the nettles have given us a fever.

Joe's getting his second wind, but despite his size he looks younger somehow, like a little lad, jog-walking beside me. Nettle rash all over his face, as bright as a blush.

He's there when I get to the gates of the caravan park. Following me like a shadow under the sign: *Happy Sands Caravan Park*. Past the launderette and past the little shop, past the postbox that's been taped up now for a year, because the Royal Mail doesn't collect from here any more.

I can feel him behind me when I get to our bungalow, me and Mam's. I turn long enough to put my arms round him. Our hearts are still beating hard as drums, blood hot. We hold each other tight for what seems like an age. I smell his sweat.

'Don't tell anyone,' he says, holding on. 'Please, Rabbit, promise me. You can't. Not your mam, not anyone.'

Then he's heading to his place. And once I've slammed the door behind me, and I'm in the cool dark of the bungalow, out of the horrid light, out of the heat, I know he's seeing that hole in his mind, and his heart's with that bloke at the bottom. Like mine is.

I start crying. Slow, quiet tears.

And later, when I'm lying on my bed – after a cold shower followed by an awkward evening with Mam, and me wearing a long-sleeve jumper to hide my arms – later, when the sky outside is dark with stars, I feel him in his grandma's place, feel his need, his fear. Feel it like it's my own. Like it's the same, all tangled up, two bunches of the same string that can't be untied.

Joe and me.

Stuck like trouble.

NINE

THINKING BACK, IT seems unreal, all of it.

Like one of my daft dreams. I start thinking about the practicalities of it all. To throw someone down a hole, shut him in like that. How could anyone – even someone as vicious as Billy – do a thing like that? Why? I can't make head nor tail of what Joe has told me – about the fires and all that. It doesn't make sense. I could well believe Billy was mad enough to burn something down, but fires at six farms? And, anyway, what exactly has it to do with Joe or the man in the hole – what was it Billy called him? *Max*?

The hole.

In the night, in my sleep, it comes back to me.

There's this impossible light inside that shines bright as torches from the bloke's bins. Bins meaning glasses, meaning specs, meaning the poor sod's sight is shot. And in a dark hole, alone, too.

In my dream, I see what's impossible to see. That's how dreams are: not real life, but something else. Like you've crossed over some threshold into a different world, the same but different. Upside down or back to front or something. I'm not sure, but Joe would know. He dreams, too, see. All his dreams, he says, are about him flying, about escape. Says he'll probably never get out of this place, so why not dream about it? For a fella who smiles a lot, there's a sadness in Joe, too, bigger than I can take in. He says he can control his dreams if he concentrates hard enough – he means that in his dreams he can choose to fly over the sea, over countries, over the Himalayas, if he wants to. And he has done. Which sounds daft to me, because how can you concentrate in your dreams? Me, I'm just helpless to watch.

Like in this one.

Here I am, staring down into that hole again, like I never left. Only now it's not day any more, not hot. And it's all real clear below me, the dark sparked alive with a sort of magical moonlight shine.

It's the bloke I see.

He's sitting under the hard light, blinking – stocky and short with a square jaw and a bit of a beard, and a mouth as straight as a nail. And this sound in the blue of it all, like a growl or something. Some animal wail. But it's not real, I tell myself. Because the wolves have gone, and for good. I know that. Gone and in the past, like Dad. And, anyway, I couldn't have seen him properly yesterday, not really. But the thing is, in that way dreams have, how I see him in my mind is almost exactly as he turns out to be. You'll see. Thick-set, and a mouth hard and straight. Shaking, he is, in the dream. Arms wrapped around his knees, hands black bright with muck, fingers taut, pulling hard on the legs of his jeans, and the knees worn through, almost. But his eyes say something different from his folded-over body. A stubbornness there, a strength. Familiar, as though I've seen it before, as though I know it.

45

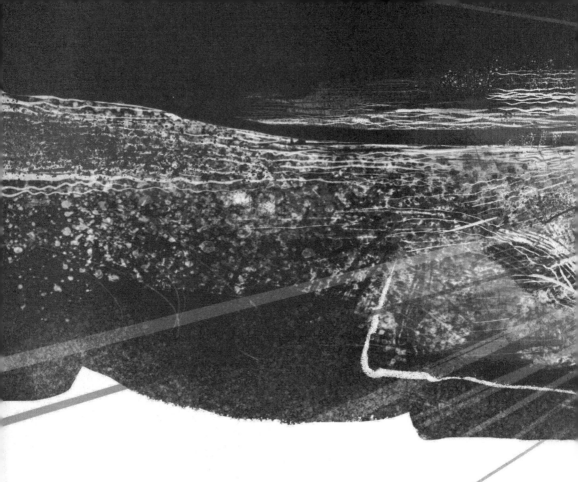

Now I'm awake and all in a lather of sweat – and that horse comes back to me. The white horse of the other dream. And the coincidence of it all is too much, which is why I haven't mentioned it to Joe, because he doesn't hold with any thoughts of coincidence. He's one for fate, he says. Everything's fated, even the dropping of a pin, he tells me. Proper superstitious, he is. Throws salt over his shoulder, salutes magpies, all that.

And maybe he's right, I think, knowing he, too, will be awake in the night right now and staring at the dark of the ceiling and thinking on that hole and that bloke and those glasses that shine bleak as broken mirrors.

TEN

IT'S STILL DARK when I climb out of bed. I've spent the last hour with my ears pricked, trying to work out if Mam's asleep, listening out for her soft snores. All evening she could tell something was wrong. 'You're quiet, Love,' she'd said. 'Trouble between you and Joe?' she'd said. 'It'll blow over,' she'd said. 'You'll see.' She's got used to biding her time with me, waiting for the right moment to ask questions. Afraid I'll have a turn again, go silent, like before. As good and gentle as any counsellor, is Mam. And she knew tonight wasn't the night.

Now she's asleep, and I'm up and pulling on my jeans. A tiptoe hush to the front door, and then I'm outside, and you can bet there's a lovely chill to the air. Not that it's cold, because it isn't. Not even close. But compared to the day it's like sitting in a cool bath. The stings on my arms itch and throb, but it's nice, if that makes sense. It wakes me up, because my head is tired with the day's thinking. I'm still not sure what it is I'm planning to do, but I know whatever it is, it won't get started with me in bed.

I go to Joe's place, look in through the windows, but careful, like. Billy's pickup is parked out front, so I know he's in there. And it's clear me tapping on Joe's window isn't an option, not tonight.

With my luck it'll be Billy who sticks his head out the door, on his way to giving me a hiding.

I text Joe.

I'm outside. Meet me at the gate. Five mins.

And then it's the wait on the road, and now the night does feel cold, although I know it's not. But I'm shaking a bit anyhow. Not with fear. Something else. Louise calls it a name I can't remember but, basically, it's like your body has its own memory, its own history, and it's one you have no hand in. And you might feel proper calm and quiet, and even your rabbit brain might be sleeping, but your body has other ideas. That's where the trauma is, she says.

Well, my body right now seems to be lost in a dance to music I can't hear. I'm thinking it's the music of the underground, of men lost down holes and horses galloping somewhere, of wolves that I thought were long gone. I try to breathe, do the exercises Louise has taught me. Slowing the blood. But I'm shaking so hard now that it feels like if I stay here like this, I'll shake myself silly. I'll get whiplash if I don't move. And there's no sign of Joe.

So what I do is I start running.

You heard me.

It's nearly one o'clock in the morning, middle of summer, and here I am running down an empty road, flanked by the blue fields on either side, and nothing ahead but more road, and it's like I'm in my own private marathon. 'Run Rabbit Run' comes into my head, something my mam used to sing to me when I was a kid.

Run, Rabbit.

And I do. I run like there's something after me. I run until my lungs burn and my legs have no feeling in them any more. I run until my eyes are near-popping out of my head. And you know what? It feels good. My body feels right. I feel like this is how I should be – running into the night, like if I don't, I'll just vanish off the face of the earth. Like as long as I'm moving I'm alive, I'm real. And the minute I stop, it'll all be over.

If I could, I'd run for ever, I'm thinking. I'd run across the moors, run down the A64, past York, and into my old town, and further on until I'm with Sophie again. Me and her. Because I miss her like you won't believe. I miss the time before, when for a short while I felt happy. Before the Scares.

And my dad, too – memories of him come back to me, and they might as well be the memories of another life. It's been so long since I've allowed myself to remember him, and suddenly I can see him here on the road. I see him walking down the moonlit road ahead of me, carrying his service pack, shoulders wide as you like, and chin held high. Large as life. Walking like he owns this land, like he was always here. Like him and the earth belong together. And now there are stags in the distance, and the sound of creatures stirring—

Time slows.

Stops.

I notice that my face is wet.

I'm crying. Running like a bastard and tears streaming down my face, too hot to stall.

And before I know it, I'm there. The farm.

I can see it on the horizon.

The Cullen place.

And all of a sudden, I know where I've been heading all this time.

The way is the same. The ditch. The fallen tree. Rusty tractor. The hill and the dip.

But it looks different at night. I wipe my face dry, and there's a stab of something in my guts, something I can't judge. Anger, maybe. Anger at Joe, at Dad, anger at the bloke in the ground.

My eyes become lost in the blue grass, like a sea so vast you can't tell where it begins, where it ends. The light on the coast isn't the same as in town where we used to live, especially at night. In summer here, the sky is never black. There are too many stars, too much moon. Everything is the same dark-bright, the same shade of twilight, like green mixed with blue mixed with colours there are no names for yet.

I seem to be wading through the first field for ever. The brush and rasp of the barley makes my hands sore. On and on it goes, and I don't even notice the tree that looks like a cow. But then the land shifts beneath me, and I lose my balance. I slide down the hill on my backside. And now the smell of rot, and here are the nettles, and the square shape of the barn against the low light.

For ten minutes or more I search the grass for the doors. In the day they shouted to be seen, but now it's like they've just disappeared. Like they were never here. I walk circles, searching for a sign of them, but there's nothing. Not even a trampled trail of our footfalls.

For a moment I think I've made the doors up. Another daft dream.

Then I see the dull gleam of the handle.

I've got a sweat on. All that running has soaked my T-shirt through, even at night. But I've never felt so full of life, so full of energy. It makes my heels bounce, and maybe that's what he hears, all the way down there, beneath the thickness of the doors. Because I don't say anything. Not a word. It's not me who starts it, but him.

'Please,' he says.

Real quiet at first, like no voice at all. Like it's the night itself talking to me, whispering in my ear. Just a single word. *Please*.

So he's alive. Because, all the way through the field I've been expecting him to be dead, that's the truth. Expected Billy and his mates to have killed him. But he's alive and he's talking to me.

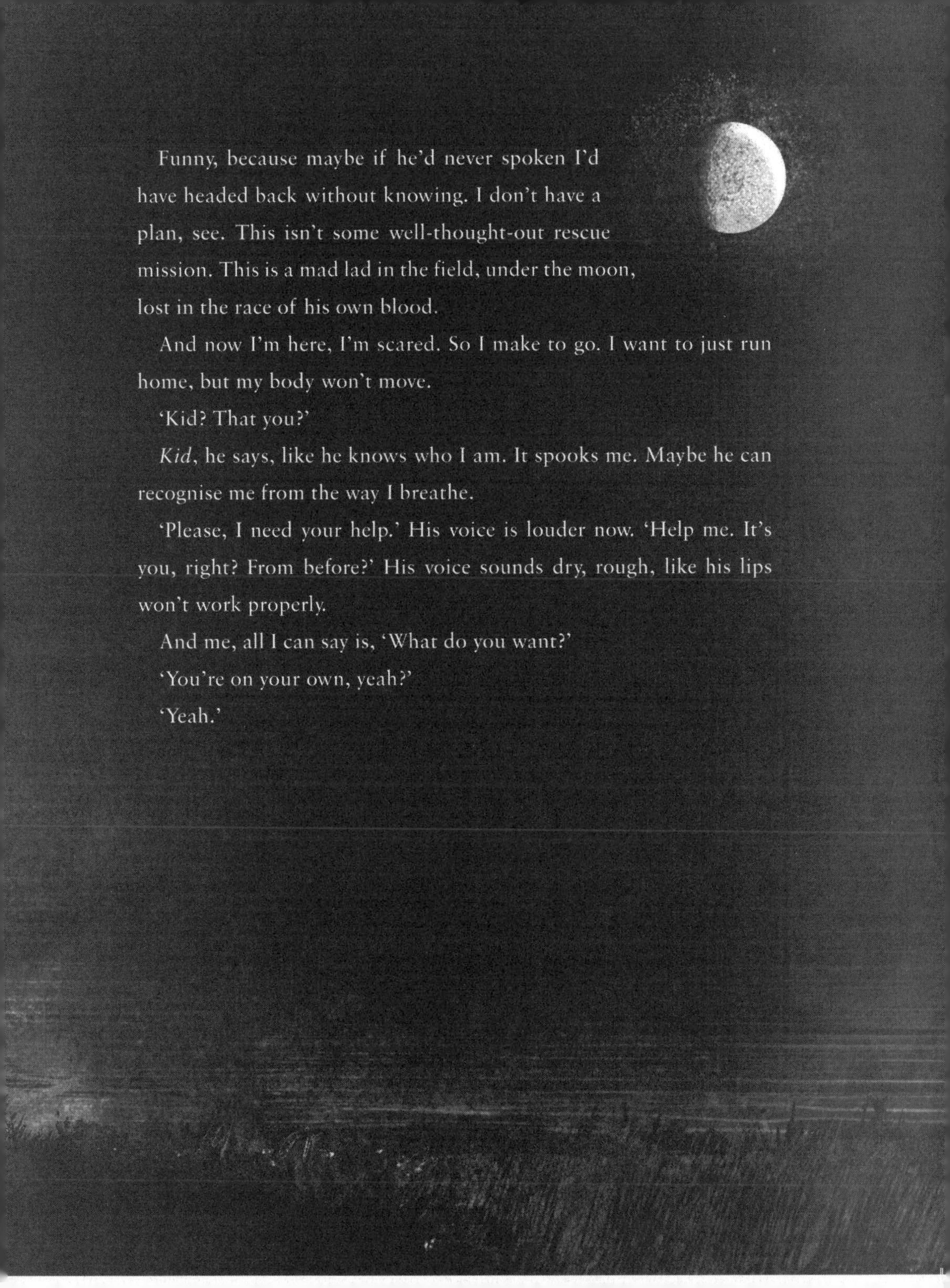

Funny, because maybe if he'd never spoken I'd have headed back without knowing. I don't have a plan, see. This isn't some well-thought-out rescue mission. This is a mad lad in the field, under the moon, lost in the race of his own blood.

And now I'm here, I'm scared. So I make to go. I want to just run home, but my body won't move.

'Kid? That you?'

Kid, he says, like he knows who I am. It spooks me. Maybe he can recognise me from the way I breathe.

'Please, I need your help.' His voice is louder now. 'Help me. It's you, right? From before?' His voice sounds dry, rough, like his lips won't work properly.

And me, all I can say is, 'What do you want?'

'You're on your own, yeah?'

'Yeah.'

'A rope or a ladder. I need to get out of here. You can get it, right?'

Standing there, my heart aches, cluttered and swollen. And there's a feeling like something stuck in my throat, like a lump of bread, not letting me breathe properly. I know the feeling. I fear it. A while since I felt it, but I know what it could mean.

I don't speak.

'Here, don't play games,' he says. 'You're a good kid, I can tell.'

I don't like being called kid, but he's not to know that, is he?

'I'm stuck down here, you see that?'

A tightness in my chest, in my throat. Panic. Shame.

'At least get me some water,' he says.

All the thoughts that had accompanied me here, carrying me up, pushing me on, have all left me now. My mind is empty. Not peaceful, but empty, like a flooded field that drains out over time, in the sun. I know the feeling from before, in the woods, with my dad when he died. I'm frozen, see. Scared. Back then, back when he needed me, I let my dad down, and here I am repeating it all over again, because if I'd ever had any idea to rescue the fella, it's vanished. I can't get him out, I know that, the doors are too heavy and the hole's too deep. I'd need a ladder, like he says, a long one, and I have nothing. Nothing but the sensation of the night breeze on my arms, raising the hairs, the call of an owl somewhere, and the man, his voice.

There.

Under my feet. Beneath the door.

And right now, he seems more alive than me.

'Don't wait,' he says, almost a smile there in the tone, sort of a fawning sound, but an edge to it, too. A new urgency. 'Tonight, yeah?'

'Not tonight,' I say, at last. 'Can't. Maybe tomorrow.'

'No, tonight. Come on.'

'Told you – I can't.'

'Give us a break – I'll be dead by tomorrow. I can't bloody breathe down here.'

And his anger breaks something in me, cuts through the fear. I can't do this, can't be here. Not tonight. I hear Louise's voice telling me to listen to my body, to protect myself.

I want to be home.

Two steps back, then three. And I'm among the nettles before he starts pleading.

'Don't go! I didn't mean it, kid. Come on, I'll die down here. Honest.'

Backwards. I'm walking backwards, my eyes on the ground, as though at any minute he'll come bursting out from under those doors and come after me.

'Can't – sorry,' I manage to say. It's a struggle to get the words out, and then they're lost in the rattle of the grass and nettles and night air, and even the moon's light seems to have a sound now. It buzzes around me and inside me, something humming, making me feel dizzy.

'Come back, please!' Then louder: 'Come back!'

ELEVEN

I'M GOING TO GO, I am. Back down the road and home. But first, I get an idea, so I cross to the barn and check its doors for a padlock. When I see there isn't one, I pull back the left-hand door, and it opens, just like that.

Inside, the place is darker than night, and so stuffy it's hard to breathe. The heat from the day has stagnated, settled like a fog, making the air thick. I can already feel a headache coming on. A bit of moon falls on an armchair, burn holes in its upholstery. I don't know what I'd been expecting, but it wasn't an armchair. Maybe tools, hay, old tractor tyres.

I see a low table, too, an old pub ashtray spilling over with cigarette butts. Four or five crushed beer cans, and another six or more flattened to the ground, a dozen empty bottles. Billy and his mates had a proper party yesterday.

The barn itself is narrow and long with windows high up on either side, just below the line of its roof. Any glass that isn't smashed or missing is caked with old paint or tar, looks like. The roof is more hole than roof, with shards of light falling in patches where the hazel tree pokes through. Piles of old newspapers stand here and there about the place, mounds of rags, car parts, coils of wire and cable and hose. And all of it stinking of something that isn't cow or any other animal for that matter, except for human, I think. The same stink as the bloke in the hole. I have a quick glance to see if there's a ladder, but there isn't. I knew there wouldn't be. That's not why I'm here.

After less than a minute, I've found what I'm looking for. There's a plastic bottle in the corner. One of those big ones that usually have white glue in them or screenwash. I unscrew the cap, give it a whiff. I'm expecting the worst, but actually it smells all right. It's empty. I carry it outside and dunk it in the bath at the corner – the cattle trough – and listen to the bubbles pop and break as I slowly fill the bottle with water.

When it's almost full, I take it to the doors in the ground. I've already worked out there's no way I can lift the door on my own, I'm not daft. 'Give us a minute,' I say.

'Thanks, kid,' he calls back. 'Thank you.'

Then I'm back in the barn, down on my haunches, hands pulling at the coils of wire and cable, wary, expecting any minute that one of them is going to cut my palm wide open. I'm testing for length. The heavier it feels, the longer it'll be, is my logic. I drag out a load of black electrical cable, must be ten metres long.

I grab a steel stanchion, this long pike-shaped thing nearly as tall as me that the farmers use for putting up temporary wire fences when grazing cattle. And then I'm back at the doors in the ground, tying the cable around the handle, tight as can be. The bloke in the hole is quiet. He doesn't ask what the bloody hell I'm doing. He just sits and waits, which I'm glad about.

I grab the steel pike, jam it under the corner of the door, until the pike's standing on end.

There's a plan. It might not be obvious if you're here watching me right now, but there is. I take the end of the cable, walk out with it towards the broken-down fence, pull it taut until I've looped the end around the thickest of the uprights. I wrap it around again, pull harder, hard as I can without tearing a muscle. I don't feel the door move, but I hear it. The steel pike slips, scrapes the timber of the door, falls deeper, which is what I was hoping for.

I tie off the cable, then head back to the doors. The steel's proper deep under the door now, deep enough so that when I lever my weight on the pike, the door wedges open a bit, then a bit more.

Smells waft out. The bloke's smell. His breath, his sweat, his piss. Stale beer.

'Jesus, kid. Nice one. Nice one,' he says. I hear the grin in his voice.

It takes some time, the whole process. I wedge open the door a bit more, then shove a rock beneath the edge, head back to the fence and pull the cable tighter, tie it off. Then back at the doors again, weight on the steel, prising the door wider. Over and over.

Three more goes and the door opens enough for me to throw in the bottle of water. And yeah, it's manky water from the bath in the field, full of dead flies probably and God knows what else. But the fella down there's happy as can be.

His glasses flash with a bit of dim moonlight when I look in. One of the lenses is broken. The side of his face looks wet with blood.

'Night,' I say. Just like that. 'Night.'

And the fella, he's too busy chugging down the water to say anything back.

Before I go, I toss the pike, and think to untie the cable and throw it over by the fence, so there's nothing to say I've been here. But later, I'm not sure if I do it. My mind can't put the memory together properly. Maybe I don't. Maybe that's my mistake. Anyway, I'm back out in the nettles, past the tree that looks like a sleeping cow, and the barley and the road, but not before promising the bloke I'll be back with rope. 'Tomorrow,' I say.

Tomorrow.

PART TWO

TWELVE

Mornings in the past, with my dad, were sunlight and shade and getting up to wash in the stream water, boil tea on a fire and listening to the woods wake. That's where we lived – in a little caravan in the woods, him and me. Not a fancy van like here on the park, but an old one, long abandoned. Which sounds barmy, I know, but it's true. For a time anyway. Before it all went to pot.

Pot meaning wrong. Meaning bad. Meaning you can't hide from the outside world for long, no matter how much you try – and he did, my dad. But it caught up with him in the end.

I'd grown up in a house, and it was still there, with my bedroom all waiting for me, even while I was with him in a caravan, living wild, and you can bet Mam wasn't happy about me being there, but they were split up by then, and I could be as stubborn as him sometimes. So she let us be. And we were happy most of the time, him and me and the woods all about, like our own small kingdom. All green with ferns and ivy and moss, and the smell like you've never smelled. Like the world was born new every day.

That's how it was. How it always will be in my head when I go back there.

It's there in my dreams, too. When I'm not dreaming about horses.

When I wake up the morning after the hole, there's a lovely second or two when I can't even remember what has gone on. Can't remember the black barn. But the bedsheets are wet with sweat, fever-heat on my skin. My head feels thick, and the funny thing is, I'm thirsty. Tongue like sandpaper. My eyes are so dry I think I hear them click when I open them. I don't have any idea what time it is, but the curtains are all lit up with sun.

Then the noise of my mobile ringing.

'Meet me on the beach, quick,' Joe's saying. 'It's Billy – he's gone mad.'

I'm still half asleep, but the force in Joe's voice wakes me, so I start going over in my head what exactly I did last night. Trying to cut through the confusion. I pull on my jeans, the same ones from yesterday, all dusty brown and stiff with dirt. Then, with barely a wave to Mam in the square as she unloads supplies for the park shop, I'm past the holidaymakers getting ready for a day out, and climbing over the gate at the cliff edge, and down the steps, heading for the beach.

Joe's been here a while. He's spent the time wandering over the sand, his footprints describing messy patterns that match his thoughts. I'm half expecting to see Billy here, too, raging. But Joe's alone.

'The bastard's gone,' he says, as soon as I'm near enough.

'Who – Billy?' The cool of the sea hits me now, like a splash of water in my face. I love this place, I'm thinking. Despite it all. I love being here with the sea spreading out before me, like it might never end. I rub my arms. The nettle rash has almost gone already, just a tingly numbness where the little red spots still shine.

'No, not Billy.' Joe's face is drawn, heavy with worry, and I'm wondering if Billy's hurt him. If something happened yesterday when we got back from the field, a fight maybe.

'Then who?' I say.

'The bloke down the hole. He got out. God knows how, but he did.' A flash of anger in Joe's eyes now. 'One of Billy's mates was there this morning, and when he looked, the hole was empty, doors wide open.'

I don't know what to say straight away. First off, I'm surprised – how did he get out of there, in his state, in the dark? His voice last night, it sounded like the voice of a man who could barely stand, barely breathe. Then I realise, I'm glad. After all, that's what we wanted, right? For him to be free?

But Joe isn't happy, not by a long chalk. He looks furious.

'It's good news,' I tell him, smiling and trying to make him smile, too. 'He's out, Joe.'

'Good news?' He spits out the words. 'You don't get it. Billy's mad enough to kill someone.'

The sea gives a chill to the air that makes your arms all goosey. We're at the far end of the beach where only the dog walkers come because the cliffs here aren't pretty. They're black slate with green slicks down them, little waterfalls slapping down from all the farm fields a mile in each direction. There's a smell of seaweed, something eggy, too, which I don't mind and neither do the seagulls, because they're floating like kites above us, squawking and making a riot.

The tourists do mind, though. The stink, I mean. So we're alone, me and Joe, and we can talk. But for some reason Joe's gone quiet now, that sheepish look has come over him again.

'What is it?' I say. 'What's up?'

'Last night, you texted me.'

'Yeah.'

'You didn't do it, did you?' he asks. I can't read him straight away, his face is sort of blank. 'Did you, Rabbit? Was it you helped him out? Say something.'

I'm going to tell him no, say it wasn't me. Because for all I know, it wasn't. For all I know the bloke got out there by magic or something. But already I'm doubting myself. Because if I did leave the cable there, then maybe—

'I went last night,' I tell him, and I look out to sea, try to catch my breath. Salt on my lips and in my eyes. Stinging and hot. 'I went, just to see he was still alive. And I gave him some water, that's all. But I swear I didn't help him out.'

Joe wheels away, makes some sort of noise, like he's sick. When he turns back to me, it's that same fear from yesterday I see. 'How could you do it, eh?' he says. 'You promised.'

'I didn't tell anyone, I swear.'

'But he's out, Rabbit. Because of *you*.'

Bad stuff gets into you, twists in your blood until you can't breathe – Pain and Grief and Guilt. I could see it now in Joe. I'd had my own share, of course, and it was still in me. What with my dad, and him dying. That was back in another place, though, another time. And some days in East Ferry, when it's a high sun and high tide, you can almost trick yourself into thinking it really is another life. Here, the skies seem to go on for ever, and there's enough air for two lifetimes. Or that's what it felt like before we found the hole. Before yesterday. But now the sunlight is acidy and yellow, and the smell of sulphur is making me feel sick.

'I tell you, Rabbit, if you got him out that hole you'll get skinned, all right. Me, too. Billy's on the warpath.' We're pounding the sand now, circling each other, both of us alive with this hot, wild energy. Joe's hand is on the sleeve of my T-shirt, pulling tight. He looks like he's going to clout me, and I'm wondering what will happen if he does, because I've never been in a fight, not a proper one. And I don't want to fight my best mate. Not Joe. 'You any idea what he'll do to me, eh?' he says.

'But you wanted him out, didn't you? That's why you showed me the hole. So he's out now, it's over, right? That's why you took me – why you lied!'

'Not like this,' he says. And I'm not sure he knows what he's saying, not altogether. But soon the anger seems to leave him, and he lets go of my shirt.

I'm slow this morning, I admit it. I'm not thinking right, and when

my thoughts do start to come together, we've made two new circles in the sand. 'So Billy doesn't know how the fella got out, does he?' I say. 'Joe, listen, if Billy had found out, you'd know about it, right? So there's no need to worry, not yet.'

'And what if they catch him?'

'So what?' I say. Then, 'Who is he anyway? Why have they got it in for him exactly?'

'A bloke Billy knew,' Joe says, all quick words again. 'He's called Max. He found out about Billy's moneymaking schemes, saw them start one of the fires. Said he was going to tell the cops.' Joe takes a breath, his voice calms a bit. 'Look, if Billy gets hold of him, this bloke's going to tell them that you were there, and it'll be me Billy blames. He'll kill me, Rabbit. The bastard will kill me this time.'

His eyes are clouded up, like he could cry. He paces across the sand, looking for some direction to head in, before stopping to face the cliff.

'This time? What do you mean *this time*?' I say, when I finally get my voice back. Because me, I've been tearing up, too. I can feel it in my throat. There's an energy here today. Not like before with Joe – not a clean, excited energy, but something deeper that needles into me, filling my lungs. 'Joe? What do you mean?'

'You don't know him,' he says. 'You don't know what he's capable of.'

'Then tell me.'

It's been something I've been wanting to ask for ages, long before any hole. Maybe he hears the eagerness in my voice, and it surprises him. He looks at me, his cheeks flushed, eyebrows salted by the air. 'He'll kill someone if he has to. That's not talk. He will. He's been setting fires all summer, just for a bit of money. Set one for a laugh, first off, and then got the idea of going round the farms, telling them him and his mates will keep an eye on their places for a fee. Thinking he was clever. Course, they didn't bite. But then he burned another down, and you better believe they changed their minds sharp.'

Joe takes a breath, rubs the palm of his hand against his eyes, like they're dry or something, like he's got sea salt in one. 'Billy didn't care if anyone was in those barns or not. So if he'll do that for a bit of cash, Rabbit, what do you think he'll do when he's angry, eh?'

'Then we'll tell someone,' I say. 'We can go to Mam. I'll come with you.'

'And what? Tell her me and Billy have been burning places down?'

I hesitate, taking it in. 'You?' I say.

Joe's shy again, quiet. And I remember what he was trying to tell me yesterday, in his rush: *I didn't want to, but Billy he—*

'He took me along for the second one, said I needed to learn how the world works. About time I made myself useful. It was this stock shed, full of old gear.' Joe's chin trembles, and he rubs it with the back of his hand. 'He made me pour the petrol. He was laughing, like it was some joke or something. Says I was old enough to do a proper night's work. Then he gave me a lighter, and told me to throw it in the barn, set it going.'

I don't want to believe it, I don't. For a moment, Joe looks so small and frightened I want to hug him. All this time he's lied, kept the full story from me. I feel stupid, childish somehow, like I've been taken in. Something in his eyes tells me that he feels worse, though.

'If Billy gets caught,' he says, 'I do, too. You get that, yeah?'

I'm about to say something when his phone goes off.

Why didn't you tell me? That's what I want to ask him. *You should never have kept it from me.* But I never get the chance.

He glances at the screen of his mobile. 'It's him,' he says, wiping his face. 'Billy. He needs me. I got to go, they're out searching for the bloke.'

'Wait—'

I've got a dozen questions I still want to ask him, but he's already heading back to the path, and then he's climbing the old, worn steps up the cliff.

'Joe – it'll be all right,' I call after him. 'It will.' But we can both hear how hollow it sounds. 'I'll help, I promise.'

'Best help you can give me is to keep quiet,' Joe says, without looking back. 'And whatever you do, stay clear of Billy.'

THIRTEEN

Something comes to my mind after Joe's gone, after I hear the roar of Billy's pickup ring out over the cliffs. A name I try to remember. One of the death spirit stories that Joe told me about once.

That's how my brain works. Blame Dad. Billy's smelling blood, my best mate's caught up in the biggest crime story East Ferry has ever known, and me, I'm thinking about creatures that don't exist again.

Kelpie. That's what it's called. I remember because after Joe told me, I'd looked it up at the library, found it in a book of legends. Something about what he said was vivid, like one of the great beasts my dad spoke about, only they had been real once, and this, well, this was just a myth.

I can remember it word for word:

> *Kelpie, being the Scottish faerie of inland and salt waters. Appears as a young horse that lets itself be ridden and tamed. On land the Kelpie is a calm, benign creature but if it reaches a river or ocean it will carry whoever rides it into the water, drowning them.*

I picture my dream again. The white horse by the sea. And I begin to wonder if the horse was as helpless as I remember.

I'm thinking all this while I wander around the park. I don't want to go home yet, don't want to have to face Mam and explain why I haven't showered, why I'm so dirty.

While she's in the office, I sneak back into the bungalow, go to my room and fall on my bed. I probably only got a couple of hours' kip last night, and the conversation with Joe has worn me out. So before I know it, I'm asleep, just like that. And the wolves, they're calling to each other in the dark and, somewhere, heavy hooves clatter the ground. Shift and slither. The sound of something scared, all frightened-up and not knowing where to go. That white horse trapped in the night, eyes wide. Its pain so shrill it makes my head hurt.

I'm there, too, in the dream. Close to her. 'Here, girl,' I'm saying, hand reaching out. 'I'm as frightened as you,' I tell her. 'I am.' And this horse, as big as anything I've ever seen, she's stumbling back and forth, and any minute she might just bolt over me and crush every bone in my body. 'Gentle,' I say. 'Gentle, girl.'

Something cracks in the night, a bang as loud as you like. Thunder or something. And then she's off, that horse, stretching over me like white fire. The weight of a planet she is, and I'm thinking I'm done for. If she misses her step, I'm dead.

Love.

But the horse just keeps going, those long white legs of hers, like bars of silver over my head, splitting the night sky—

'Here, love!'

Mam?

Now I'm awake, and stumbling up. I hear her out front. Know her footsteps better than I know my own.

Bang bang of a door.

'Get out here, come on. Shift yourself.' Mam's voice bouncing like headlights across the hall outside. Then she's at my door: 'There's work to do.'

After I've washed and changed my clothes, I'm out in the square, emptying the litter bins, proper glamorous work, when Joe's gran shouts me over to hers.

Win's sunning herself at her white garden furniture, just a chair and a table, with a clutter of creams and other stuff she likes to daub on herself. Likes the sun, does Win. Shorts and a vest and no bra from May until October, and sunspots on her arms so deep you can barely make out the small tattoos of a swallow and a bee.

'You and Joe had a falling out?' she asks, her eyes closed and face tilted to the sun. Her voice, soft as kidskin. Like I said, she's called Win, Joe's gran. Short for Winny, which is short for Winifred, which must have been an old woman's name long before she was even born.

'No. Why?' But I answer too quickly, maybe, and she opens her eyes, and aims this sharp look at me, weighing things up. She's cool, is Win, gentle and calm as you like, but when she winks you guess there's stories to be told from her past that would make you blush, if only she'd tell. Never angry, is Win, always smiling. Loves Joe and is wary of Billy, but doesn't show it. Likes me, too, or seems to. Kind, and never a bad word about anyone, so you'd never guess Bastard Billy was related to her.

'You get used to lads' moods when you live in a house of them,' she says. 'And Joe's been worked up since yesterday. You wouldn't know anything about that?'

I shake my head. I don't like lying to Win, but what choice have I got?

'Maybe he's caught it from Billy,' she says, 'because he's in one of his dog moods, too.'

I just stand there, shielding my face from the sun with a hand, and she takes me in. And maybe she knows whatever nervous energy is working its way through Joe is in me, too, because she seems to cut me some slack. Turns back to the sun and closes her eyes.

'Well, whatever it is, make sure you lads stick together, OK? Nothing's worth losing a friendship over. And Joe needs you more than you think, Rabbit.'

I spend the rest of the morning helping Mam clean out some of the vacated vans, and Joe, he comes back about midday — I can see him sitting out by the cliff, keeping away from me, it looks like. A bit later him and Win make their way down to the beach and back. Win looks up and waves at me as they go, but Joe pretends he hasn't seen. While they're gone, I notice Billy's pickup pull in to park at their bungalow. Billy and another bloke, both of them real hectic, slamming the doors of the truck and rushing into Win's place like they've got a fire under them. Me, I get that hollow feeling inside of me again. I'm just about ready to abandon Mam and run to Joe, tell him they've cottoned on to us, found out what we did, when Billy reappears. He's holding another box of beer he's pulled from Win's fridge, and he stops by the pickup and lights a fag. Then him and the other bloke say something to each other, both of them looking like there's a real bad smell under their noses, something dead and rotting.

Me and Mam are up at one of the long-term rental vans, up behind the laundry, but I can see him from the decking, plain as day. He's angry. You can feel it from this distance, it's coming off him thick as smoke. He turns, and now he sees me. He squints and makes this little nod of his head, like he's signalling something to me. A warning, maybe. And I'm thinking any minute now he'll march up here, grab me by my scruff and ask me why I was at the hole, and where's the bloke?

But all he does is get back in the pickup, and him and his mate accelerate down the lane and onto the road.

I stand there at the door of the vacant van, staring, until the sound of the pickup fades into the low, heavy noise of the scorching fields in the distance.

'Here,' Mam says, breaking the spell, 'are you helping with this or not? Where's your head at today?' Two bin bags in her hands, and me in the way. 'Take these, then you can start on number forty-six. Hasn't been cleaned since Mrs Wickman.' Mam's eyes on mine, sensing the worry in me. 'You're OK, aren't you?' And I nod quickly, and she knows not to wait to ask a second time.

FOURTEEN

THINGS CAN GO bad real quick. I've seen it for myself, with Dad. With how he got dragged down into trouble, and then before you can work out why it all happened, he's dead. Too late for guilt and second thoughts.

That's what the hole is for Joe, I'm thinking. This point in time where things change for the worse. But I don't know the half of it, because there's more trouble to come. Seems like there's a never-ending supply of it, when all you want is a bit of time to breathe. And when it does come, you can bet trouble usually arrives in the form of a man, which is how it happens to me this time.

Up at forty-six.

Maybe I'm so caught up in Billy and *his* danger, that I'm deaf to any other sort. Because I don't notice, see, don't even think about what danger might already be here on the park.

It's one of the residential vans, meaning it's not for holidays but for living in. Long and coffee-coloured with a vanilla stripe. It has this fancy decking round the front, a handful of plants in terracotta pots. It's been empty since Mrs Wickman passed away four months ago, and it will stay like that until her family stop arguing over her will. Which may be never, given what they're like.

But this week they've asked us to clean it, keep it trim while they wait to sell it.

So there's no one living there, I know that, and Mam says she left the place unlocked earlier.

I try the handle, though, and it doesn't give. It's like there's something pulling at the door from the inside, jamming it shut. And me, I don't think anything's dodgy, see, don't suspect. I walk around the back, looking in at the windows. The curtains are all closed. I glance back to the lane that runs to the little square with the shops and the office, back the way I came. Back home.

I'm still looking, when I feel a hand clap around my mouth, and a second one goes around my throat.

I smell him before I see him. He smells of the hole, and all of a sudden it's like I'm back there.

My rabbit brain's firing off adrenalin all over. But this is real fear, I tell myself. This is real danger. No dreaming, no Scares.

'Don't you dare try anything. If you do, you'll know about it, understand? I don't want to hurt you, but I will,' he says. 'Nod your head.'

It's not easy nodding your head with two hands holding you still. But I do it.

'Good kid. Here—'

He drags me backwards, up the stairs, onto the decking. Drags me so hard, I lose my footing and he just drags me harder, and I'm thinking, in the hole he didn't look that big. No bigger than me, and here he is pulling me like a sack of flour. Because I knew who it was, long before he called me kid. And the scary thing is, he knows me, too.

Mrs Wickman's old place has patio doors, and he kicks them open and takes me inside.

'Down!' he yells.

I'm thrown to the carpet while he messes with the doors, trying to get them to shut, then he pulls the curtains closed.

It's dark inside, stuffy. I can hear my heart beating, hear my lungs rasp. There's this whining sound in my ears, and it's like I'm in the woods again, in the ferns, and the sound of beasts somewhere under me, scrabbling, fighting to get out.

The noise of them is so loud I don't hear him the first time he says it. So he has to ask again, which just makes him crazier.

'I said, what's your name?' He's bearing down on me, the collar of my T-shirt bunched in his fist. He's not yelling, he's hissing. This real low sort of hiss, and I can't work out if he can't talk or if he's just trying to sound hard. 'Name, kid.'

'R-Rabbit,' I tell him.

'What?'

It's too dark to see his expression. The curtains are terracotta, like the pots on the decking, and they glow with the sun outside. The furniture in here is all pine and orange fabric. Everything a hot reddish orange, like the colour when you close your eyes on a real sunny day. Walls cluttered with Mrs Wickman's watercolour scenes of the coast. The pictures shake in the dark every time the bloke moves.

I'd been in here once since the old lady died, just to look with Mam, but not like this.

'Rabbit. My name's Rabbit.'

It's the first time I hear him laugh, and I'm not sure if it's a laugh at all, or if he's clearing his throat. 'So, that your mother down at the office, Rabbit?'

I nod.

'You live here on the park?' His throat's real dry, lips cracked, making his voice hard to understand. There's a wheezing noise when he breathes. And his eyes behind those broken specs, they're wide and white. A crack like a spider's web in his left-hand lens.

Nod.

'She in charge, your mother?'

'Here, I won't—' I'm only going to tell him that I'm not gonna cause him any bother, that I'll do what he says, but his hand claps to my mouth before I can get the words out.

'*Quiet.*'

He holds it there for a few seconds, his eyes sort of screwed shut, thinking, then . . .

'Please,' he says under his breath. Another few seconds pass, the sound of his lungs working, a wet sound in his chest. 'Look, if I take my hand away, you won't yell, right?' he whispers. 'I told you, no noise, please. Do what I say, yeah?' He slowly lifts his hand from my mouth. His face – I can see it better now. It's alive with shock and worry. And I see the wound on his forehead, a bit of blood, the skin grazed away.

His arm, the left one, is
sort of limp, and there's
more blood on his sleeve, a lot of it. He's panting now as he leans
away from me. Looks like he might collapse, but then he's straightening
up, and he stares directly at me. 'Promise,' he says.

'I promise.'

'I need some food, something to drink,' he says. 'You can take it
from the shop down there, can't you? And any money that's in the till,
got it?'

'She'll notice if I take any money,' I say, real quiet, so he doesn't hurt
me again. 'But I've got fifty quid saved from the work I've done. Not
much, but some.'

'I won't take a kid's money.' He squeezes his eyes shut, again, like
he's got a bad head. Feels his way to the end of the sofa, then sits there
looking sort of embarrassed and proud at the same time. It's like the
wind's been taken out of him. The bluster's gone.

'I can get you food, no problem,' I say, without getting up from the floor. 'Frozen chicken, pizza. I can bring it here.'

'Yeah,' he says, thinking. 'And get the electric and water connected to this place. Can you do that?'

I nod.

'Thanks. And the keys to this van,' he says, turning to me, blinking. 'Leave it all outside the door tonight, before midnight, yeah?'

I'm still sitting on the carpet, and seeing me, something shifts in his eyes. He bends forward and tries to pull me up to my feet.

'You all right?' he asks, a bit of shock in his voice, like he doesn't know what's happened, how I ended up down there. Like he wasn't the one who did it. Like the last few minutes never happened.

I say I am. I think I am. I'm not hurt, if that's what he means.

I want to ask him what's wrong with him, because he's not right, I can see that. Maybe it's the knock on the head he took, or the trough water I gave him to drink made him ill. He's wet with sweat, his hair matted in grease. Looks a proper sight, almost bad enough to pity. 'You need a doctor,' I say.

He shakes his head. 'I'm fine,' he says. As if to prove the point, he climbs to his feet, but it takes a while, and when finally he's up, his voice hardens. 'And don't get the police involved or anyone else, understand?'

I say I do, but his face tells a different story. He's trying to sound like a hard case, but it isn't in him. He's just parroting words he's seen in films. He looks so weak, he might collapse any moment.

He's staring at the patio doors, and he's boiling with a fever. His fear filling the dead woman's caravan, so bitter it's like there's no air left. Then his eyes dart down to his torn jeans, the bloody shirt.

'I – I suppose I'll need a towel, some clothes.'

'There's some of my dad's old things. I can bring you them.'

'Whatever fits,' he says, adding, 'thanks.'

Two thank yous in as many minutes. He's pretty polite for a hard case, I'm telling myself. He goes to open the patio doors, to let me out, but thinks twice, that panic in him rising. I feel it, smell it on him. I know the smell of panic, all right. 'I'm not a bad man,' he says then, 'I swear. Sorry if I hurt you.'

And me, I don't know what to say to that, because what do you say to a bloke who just tried to throttle you and then says sorry? So I say nothing.

'Tonight then, Rabbit, OK?' he says, finally, and I nod.

Then I'm outside with the fresh air on my face, and the dead woman's caravan behind me.

FIFTEEN

I DON'T HEAR from Joe for the rest of the day. No replies to my texts, no knock on the bungalow door.

It's way past midnight before I manage to get back to the van.

Mam stays up late, and when she finally goes to bed, I sneak into the living room, and take the keys for the shop from her bag. I can't leave yet, though. Not yet. Not until she's deep sleeping. So I go back to bed and I get the mobile and text Joe, hoping he's awake. Joe still doesn't know that the bloke's here in the park. And me, I don't know what to tell him, how much I can say by text, but I just want to know he's safe, that him and me are all right. What Win said has spooked me a bit.

Still no reply. So I get the clothes out of the spare room. There are jumpers, jeans, old pairs of khaki combats, some socks, boots. Mam's kept quite a bit of Dad's stuff – she never stopped loving him, despite it all – but no way am I giving anything good to some dying bloke I don't know. So I grab some old gear he barely wore and shove it in a bag.

It's almost two in the morning when I get outside, and the sky is filled with a dull silver, like sheet metal. Everything around is a silhouette, including the van on the hill.

The shop's no bother. I know the alarm code, and it only takes me a couple of minutes to pack a carrier bag with chips and bread and chicken steaks. I put in a can of beer, too, some crisps. Then I'm outside forty-six. I place the bag down on the decking, tap on the patio doors twice, but quiet. I've brought the money I'd saved as well. There's only just over thirty quid, instead of fifty, but it's something, isn't it? Enough to get him on his way, if he's got it in him.

The door opens wide enough for me to squeeze through, and then I'm inside.

'Thanks for turning on the electric,' he says, already taking the bag off me. 'Did you get everything?' Despite how bad he is, at least he hasn't been daft enough to put on the light, in case Mam sees. But he's got the fridge door open, and by its little bulb I can see him emptying the bag onto the carpet. He crosses to the microwave in the corner of the kitchen area and puts something inside. There's some energy in him that wasn't there before, and I'm guessing he's managed a few hours' sleep. 'Where are the keys?' he says, still holding the shopping bag. 'The keys to this van, do you have them?' he whispers.

'I can't get them. They're in the office, in the cabinet. Mam knows the combination, not me.' Which is all true.

I expect him to be angry, but he just has this real placid look on his face. He puts on the striplight above the kitchen top, and I can see the wound on his forehead now, near his left eye, another bit of blood where the glasses cut him. Bruises on his cheek, too. It's young, his face, much younger than Mam, not much older than Billy, probably. But there are lines under his eyes, like being scared has taken its toll on him. I get the feeling this fella has been scared for a long time.

'The water's not working,' he says, and as he says it, his eyes sort of soften. Like a boy's eyes. He takes a step away from me, seems embarrassed at being so filthy. He slides his dirty hands beneath his armpits.

'You have to turn the stopcock on. It's under the van. I'll do it after. Here,' I give him a small bottle of water that I've had stuffed in the back pocket of my jeans. It's from our fridge and cold.

He grabs at it, desperate, and I step back away from him real quick, let him swig on the bottle in peace. I watch his Adam's apple going up and down like mad under the scrub of his beard. His throat is stained dark with sweat and dirt, the same colour as a conker.

'Where's the other lad?' he says, once he's finished the bottle. 'Your mate. There were two of you the other day, weren't there?'

'I'm on my own.'

Something swims in his eyes, behind those glasses of his. Something neither good nor bad, just foggy, like moonlight in November. He's seeing me but not taking me in fully, and I'm wondering if he's ready to collapse or worse, and what will I do then?

'You believe in fate?' he asks. I don't say anything, because fate's Joe's business, not mine, and he says, 'How many caravan parks are there around here, and I end up at yours? Couldn't believe it when I saw you with your mam yesterday.'

'Small world,' I say.

'Are they about?' he asks. I'm confused for a second, then from the worried look I know he means Billy and the others. The blokes who held him.

I nod.

'Near?'

'Yeah. But I'll keep a look out, though,' I say. 'If you like I'll let you know when the coast is clear, so you can go.' There's hope in me, you see. Even now. That he'll go. That me and Joe will be safe.

'Did they follow me here?'

'No. One of them lives on the park. Billy Fludde.'

'Billy? Shit.' He laughs to himself, but a pained laugh, followed by disbelief, like I've told the sickest joke he's ever heard. 'He's here, at the park? Are you with him then? One of them?' he asks. His eyes clear a bit, and he narrows them on me. There's a wince as he speaks, and he's holding himself funny, all leaning to one side, like his ribs are hurting him.

'If I was one of them I wouldn't be helping you, would I?'

I end up sounding harder than I mean to, and he goes humble again. And that makes me feel guilty, so I say, 'I got you these, too.' I take a couple of strips of paracetamol out of my pocket, hand them to him. 'You looked hurt.'

'Well, Billy's a vicious bugger,' he says, popping the first strip. 'You got any more water?'

'There's a beer in the bag.' I watch as he bends down, cracks the can and takes a swig, swallows a couple of pills. 'So what's your name?' I ask. 'Max, is it?'

The microwave pings. He moves to it, opens the door. He picks up the hot chicken steak in his fingers, drops it quick on the counter.

Then he gets two slices of bread, puts the chicken between them and starts eating. He's wearing this shirt, and you can hardly see the check on it for the dirt. Bloodstain down one side, so dark and dry it's brown instead of red.

'Sorry. You want some of this?' he asks, after he's halfway through it. Near starving himself and he's offering me a bite. 'You eaten anything?'

I nod.

'You look skinny. Where's your dad?' he asks.

'Dead.'

Most people, when I tell them my dad's dead, they look sad, and nod and act proper bereft, like they knew him themselves. And I have to take it in, like I recognise what they're going through and isn't it a shame. But this fella, he just looks at me and keeps on chewing. 'Wasn't much use as a dad, eh?' he says, like he's seen something in my face, some sign of neglect he recognises. Like we have a connection, him and me. Which we don't. Whatever it is, I don't like it, and I don't like anyone talking bad about Dad, either, and there's plenty that still do.

'He was good enough,' I say.

The bloke frowns. He takes another bite of chicken. 'My name's Maximo.'

I'm still feeling a bit pissed off about the thing with my dad, but the way he says it – *My name's Maximo* – real straight-faced, changes my mood suddenly. I know it sounds wrong – here I am with a man who looks like he's just climbed out of a grave, and I'm smiling. I can't help it because I've never known anyone called Maximo.

'What kind of name's that?' I say, with a laugh, but a careful laugh because this bloke could be a proper nutter. Could be as bad as Billy, because I don't know. 'Sounds like a magician. The *Great* Maximo.'

He frowns. 'I don't think a kid who goes by a daft name like Rabbit can criticise, do you?' he replies, chewing. He's smiling now, though, as best as he can given the state of his face. 'I can't call you Rabbit, it's stupid. What's your proper name?'

'Johnny,' I say, a bit embarrassed, because the truth is I've never liked my name. Johnny's a kid's name, I think. Not that Rabbit's any better, I'll give you that. But still. 'I'm named after my dad. He was called John. John Hill.'

Max nods, and now he does get that look – the sad look. And I'm dreading him telling me how sorry he is to hear my old man's dead. Only he doesn't. Instead he steps over to the sofa, lowers himself down, real careful, and then he says, 'Chip off the old block, right?'

'Yeah,' I say, 'something like that.'

More than you think, I want to tell him.

More than you think.

SIXTEEN

He wipes his free hand on the thigh of his jeans and reaches for mine, shakes it. 'Hello, Johnny Hill,' he says. 'Maximo isn't my proper name, either,' he adds. 'It's just what I used at the circus. But you can call me Max, anyhow.'

I'm not sure if I've heard him right. 'You worked at the circus?'

The bloke, Max, looks at me, puts down his chicken sandwich. 'For a few years now, yeah. Since leaving school.' He's quiet suddenly, looks tired. The beer and the food have gone to his head too quick. He's sitting, holding himself real careful, like he doesn't know which knackered bit he needs to protect the most. Any second now, he's gonna fall asleep, I'm thinking. Or maybe he's going to be sick.

I say, 'Look, I got your clothes.'

I cross towards him, onto the carpeted bit of the van. I notice the stains. Dark boot prints all around – looks like when Max wasn't sleeping, he spent the day pacing. I'm holding the shopping bag with the clothes in. I lift it up, in case he hasn't noticed it before now. But he isn't even looking. His eyes are closed tight. 'They should fit,' I tell him. 'You can go now then, I suppose. I could keep a look out for you.'

He couldn't even make it to the door, never mind leave the park, and I see as much. He's started to breathe funny, panting. A bit of panic rises up in me, seeing how bad he's turned, and so suddenly.

'Wait. I'll go turn the stopcock, get you some water,' I say, glad for the excuse to be out of the van for a bit.

He says nothing. He's slumped now, his chin almost on his chest. And as I make my way outside and round the back of the place, I feel the hammer in my blood again, because if I don't do something I get the feeling this bloke could die any time. But what is it that I can do? I don't even know what's wrong with him.

The stopcock is no bother, and then I'm back inside. I fill a glass of water and carry it over, and I'm not joking, I actually have to lift it to his chin, help him drink, he's that out of it. Like feeding a baby or something. But once he's got the water down, he sort of revives, opens his eyes.

'Sorry,' he says, 'I haven't eaten for a while.' His words are slurred. He takes off the glasses, rubs his face. He sits for a bit, getting his breath back. 'You – you must want me gone quick, yeah?'

'Something like that.'

'Don't blame you.'

'It's just – if Billy finds out, then there's going to be trouble. But I can help you,' I say, and I nod at his bloody shirt. 'I can bring a first aid kit. Or call an ambulance.'

'*No*,' he says, and it's the first time he's raised his voice all night. 'Not an ambulance. I told you, I'll be all right. Once I've got clean, I'll be OK.' He grimaces a bit, like something deep inside is grinding together. Maybe he's broken some bones. Then he begins to see sense. 'But a bandage might be good, some antiseptic.'

I stare at his face. Black in the lines under his eyes, like it'll never wash off. Lips cracked and raw. And his skin all sheened with fever. I can feel the heat coming from him. 'What did he do to you?' I ask, once I've brought him a second glass of water.

'Billy?' Max sips it, hands the glass to me to put down on the carpet. He lifts up the tail of his shirt, and I see a dark patch on his side, on his ribs, but I can't tell if it's blood or bruising. 'I found out what they were doing, with the fires, but they caught me before I could tell anyone. Took my mobile, my money, beat me up, threw me down the hole. He likes to kick, that fella. Could have been a footballer if he'd put his mind to it.' He winces, lets out a big breath. 'I don't want to cause you any bother,' he says. 'I'd like to go, honest. It's just not that easy.'

'Why not?'

He stares at me now, and does his best to clean his glasses on his shirt, slowly, like every motion sends another pulse of pain through his hands. Goes back to his sandwich, or tries to, because it looks like his appetite has gone all of a sudden. 'They've got something of mine. I need it back.'

'What, your mobile? It's all right, I can give you my old one—'

'I'm gonna need *my* mobile,' he says, 'if Billy hasn't sold it yet or thrown the thing. But anyway, I wasn't talking about that. It's something else, something more important. I won't be able to go till I get it back.'

I don't understand what he's saying, not a bit. It's like this bloke – this Max – wants to stay here and get killed.

'Like money?' I say.

'Better than money,' he says, swallowing hard. This sick look comes over him, and he puts the sandwich to one side. Then he's leaning heavily against the sofa back, and a moment later he's lying flat down with his eyes closed, and I'm trying to dribble a bit of the water into his mouth, see if it'll wake him up. But he bats the glass away, weakly, like he's done in and nothing's gonna stop him sleeping. 'More important,' he whispers. 'Means more to me, anyway.'

I'm thinking it must be gold or diamonds he's after, my mind going around like this is some daft story, something Joe might come up with. Treasure, and his name in the papers.

'What's is it?' I say, at last. But Max looks like he's not going to answer. He's sleeping, or passed out or something. And then his mouth moves a bit, and what he says makes my mind reel.

'A horse,' he says, his voice sinking so deep I can barely hear it. 'Billy stole my horse.'

SEVENTEEN

Dreams are never just dreams, I always knew that. Dad did, too.

Folk will tell you that it's all nonsense, and why do you fill your head with make-believe? Adults mostly, who've forgotten how to imagine, how to feel, how to love, some of them. But like those wolves in the past – which weren't just dream wolves, I can tell you, even if Louise doesn't believe me – well, like those wolves, it just so happens that it's the bloke's horse I've been dreaming about all this time.

And it's real. The horse is *real*.

'He's where?' Joe stares at me, disbelieving. This is later, once we've met on the cliff, him and me, the sun coming up and a proper beautiful morning starting.

'I've told you,' I say, but I tell it a second time, anyway – how the bloke from the hole is here on the park. How he caught me, how he looks half dead. I don't mention the horse, not yet. Not to Joe. There's enough for him to take onboard.

'Jesus,' Joe says.

It's still early, everyone in bed but me and him. Deep blue sky, and growing brighter every minute. I left Max sleeping on the sofa, a couple more paracetamol inside him. Troubled sleep, and him mumbling something that I couldn't catch. Delirious.

'He can't even stand straight, never mind leave the park,' I tell Joe. 'Billy broke his ribs, and he's got a fever. If we're gonna get rid of him, we'll need to get him better first.' I tell Joe my plan – how him and me can take shifts in looking after Max, make sure he's fed and watered, and I'll see if I can get him well, clean those wounds of his, bandage him up. Then in a day or two or three, he can get going.

Joe nods at it all, but I can't tell if he's agreeing or just trying to take it in. Two days seems like a long time with Billy sniffing about. Three seems like for ever right now.

We've moved from the spur of the cliff to sit on the fence nearby. From here you can just about see the roof of forty-six, the back of it. And we're looking towards it, just looking, that's all. There's a breeze, and the air smells real briny. Sea as calm and clear as a mirror. It's a proper lovely morning, I'm thinking, and isn't that ironic, eh?

'We've got to get him off the park,' Joe says.

'That's what I'm telling you,' I say. 'We can, but not today.'

'If Billy finds him—'

He doesn't finish the sentence. But his face says enough.

'We will, Joe, I promise,' I say. 'In a few days.'

There's a long pause, and we both feel this unspoken thing between us, big as a wall. Something we can't get over, not until we admit it's there.

So, finally I say: 'Joe, tell me, yesterday when you said he'll kill you this time – what did you mean?'

Last time I asked the question I'd rushed him, but now I'm quiet, because sometimes with people it's like winning the trust of a deer. Dad was good at it, which was odd because you'd think, looking at him, that he had no patience and no quiet inside, except for the boiling sort of quiet that fuels men like him. But when there was a young deer about, he'd hunker down in the ferns and just wait, calm as you like. Eyes on the eyes of the fawn. Soft eyes, he'd say. Like having soft hands to catch a cricket ball. Because if you caught a cricket ball wrong you'd know about it and have the bruises for days. So you need to move with the trajectory of the ball, not against it. Let the ball slip into your hands, cradle it.

'See,' he'd tell me, 'this is the same. Soft eyes. Let the fawn find you, let her make her way to you, and you just follow her, fit to her rhythm.'

And Joe's a young deer right now, and
I know that no matter how much
I care about him, the wrong
word will frighten him off.

EIGHTEEN

A MINUTE PASSES.

We sit up here, with the soft noise of the sea behind us, the beach below. The tide's coming in now, but when it's out you can walk all the way to East Ferry, following the cliffs. Real deep beach in places. There's old wrecks of ships standing up from the sand and jagged rocks like toppled buildings. Iron ships, and wood. Me and Joe – that's our playground, we say. Everything here, everything we can see, is ours.

Today, though, it seems very small. Lazy waves sliding against the rocks. Quiet. And I'm quiet, too. Waiting. Patient. Like Dad.

Joe looks thoughtful. We've never really talked about it, me and him. I mean, what goes on between him and Billy. Only what a bastard Billy is, that's all. But nothing more than that. But I know there's something Joe hasn't been able to say, won't say. Part of me doesn't want to hear it, because I'm scared of the stories he'll tell.

'He wouldn't kill you, would he?' I ask, when Joe still hasn't said anything. 'He is your brother at the end of the day.'

Joe opens his mouth, but there are no words. Just this horrible blankness to him. It's another minute before he speaks. 'He hates me, Rabbit. He does, proper hate. I think he hates everyone, but me especially. Always has.' He takes a breath, like his chest won't work properly, like his lungs are tight. 'Says I have a different mam than him, says right from the start I was a runt. Says you can tell. Like when a sow gives birth, and all the little piglets are all running about and stuff, but how there's always one that's weak and feeble. And that's me, he says.'

'That's bollocks.'

We're sitting side by side, our shoulders touching. Every now and then I glance at the side of his face, but he doesn't look at me. Eyes fixed on his hands in his lap, picking at the skin down the side of his nails with his thumb.

'He's a bully, that's all,' I say. 'Bullies are cowards, aren't they?'

It was Dad who told me that, and I believe it, because it's true enough. I know, because I'd had bullies at school, back in my old town. But bullies can still hurt and damage and break stuff, and I know that, too.

'It's not just that,' Joe says. 'He's destroyed everything I ever liked. Even when I was a nipper – if there was a toy I liked, he'd just come and break it in half. Snapped my arm once, too. Says it was an accident, but he seemed real pleased with himself after.' I look at Joe, but his face is still. There's no feeling there while he's talking. It's like he's telling someone else's story, not his own. I want to hold his hand, but I don't want to disturb the moment, so I just listen. 'We had a kitten once, Nan and me. I got real close to it, probably the only thing I ever loved, and then one day it was just gone. He said he had nothing to do with it, but I know who was behind it, all right.'

Now, a tiny flicker in his eyes. Subtle, but if you know him like I know him, you can see something shift behind the mask. His guard being lifted.

'He – he used to do this thing at night,' Joe says, his voice real low. 'When I was younger, before he went into the nick for the first time. He'd come into my room, and he'd climb onto my bed, legs either side of me, pinning my arms down. And he'd take the pillow and put it over my face, pressing until I couldn't breathe.'

I'm listening, and I notice I'm holding my breath. Like I'm there with Joe in the bedroom of his memory. I can feel the tension in his body, like he's vibrating next to me, like there's electricity in him.

'He'd keep pressing the pillow hard against my face, holding it there, pushing down. Thing is, he'd be laughing while he did it. I'd hear him. After a while, I'd stop fighting, because I can't get him off me, I just can't. He's twice my size. So I hold my breath and decide to

wait until he gives up, gets bored. Except I don't know if he ever will. A minute goes by, and my lungs are emptying out. And I'm hoping he'll stop soon, because if he doesn't I'll—'

I say nothing. Sometimes there's nothing you can say.

'So, see, I know one day he'll do it,' Joe says, and now he looks at me. 'You see, he's been practising for years.' His eyes are shimmering wet. Steady and shining and just looking at me. 'If I don't get away from him, Billy will kill me.'

Joe's shoulders swell as he takes a breath. I put my hand on the back of his neck, gentle. Holding him. He's not crying, but he's as close to it as I've ever seen him. That's when I notice the bruise under his T-shirt, near his collarbone. Proper black bruise. Deep and fresh.

Billy.

I look at it and I'm not really hearing any more. Images in my head of Billy and Joe, the bastard hitting him, holding him down.

'When I say anything, he tells me I'm lucky he just uses his fists,' Joe continues, 'because he's got a decent knife, too. And he shows it to me whenever he can.'

I'd seen the knife myself – stuck into Billy's belt, under his coat. Some days he'd walk around with it on show, like he was tempting someone to ask him about it. Small thing, kind of knife the fishermen in town wear, not much bigger than a pen knife, but sharp enough.

While we sit there, the terns about us are getting all worked up, the morning routine. They're screeching, wheeling about the cliffs. Making a right racket. It suits my mood, because my head is full of noise right now, and it's not just in my head but in my body, too. All that prehistoric memory bubbling up in me that Louise talks about. I'm getting that urge to run again, a desperate need to move, so I jump down from the fence, and when I do, Joe comes after me. We're high up, on the highest point of the cliff, and I'm not too bad with heights usually, but today I get that hollow feeling I get when I'm swimming in the sea. In the pit of my stomach, like floating. This hollow, empty feeling, like I'm becoming weightless.

It's not vertigo. I know what it is. It's my love for him. For Joe.

Because he's hurting, and I don't want him to hurt any more.

'We'll get out of here, you and me,' I say. 'It's just like you say – we're aliens round here. So we'll get out, go to college together or university or something.'

Joe laughs. Wipes his eyes dry and laughs a proper laugh. Some of that electricity eases in the air. 'I'm no good at school, you know that.'

'I'll help you. We'll get out of this place together, yeah?'

'Joe Fludde and Rabbit Hill, eh?' he says. 'Aliens. Like David Bowie – but without the funny eyes.' Joe's smiling. And I'm smiling, too, now.

Truth is, I don't have a clue how any of this might happen. Not yet. Right now what we need to do is get the man out of the van and away. That's the first thing. And dreams of uni later.

'Joe, Max said something about a horse.' I'm thinking of leaving it there, letting Joe tell me in his own time. But he's looking timid, is Joe, like he wants to hide. So I say, 'There is a horse, isn't there? I mean, you weren't lying.'

'I don't lie all the time,' Joe says, trying to sound cheerful, and not quite making it. 'Only half the time.'

'You saw it?'

He nods. 'Once. When Billy took me to the hole that time. It was there then.'

'Is it alive?'

Joe says nothing.

'It's Max's horse, isn't it? Belongs to him.' A breeze rolls over us, makes our skin prickle. Day's almost here. 'What's Billy done with it?'

Joe takes a moment. He looks pale today, sort of faint in the air, like if the wind blew up it might carry him off his feet. 'He's hanging onto it. Thinks he can sell it, maybe. Why?'

'Because if you want Max gone, he's gonna need it back.'

'Is that what he said?'

I nod. 'He's not going anywhere till he has his horse.'

Joe stops, and looks at me. 'What if he's lying? Maybe he's just trying to get more money off you?'

'No, he's all right,' I say, and I surprise myself, because I believe it, despite it all. 'He is. I think he's decent. Anyway, I don't think money means a lot to this bloke.'

'What makes you the expert?'

I want to say because I've seen it before, in my dad. Seen the same self-defeating stubbornness. The same look on his face. The same destructive drive. And with Dad, it killed him. With Max, I don't know – but I can see he's not giving up until he gets his horse, whatever it takes. That's what I want to say.

Instead I say nothing, just stand there with the wind about me, and the gulls screaming overhead. But maybe Joe sees it all anyway, in my eyes. Maybe he sees the hurt there, the memory of a body in the woods, because he says, 'You know helping him won't bring your dad back, right?'

I nod, but there's a sting behind my eyes, an ache. 'I know.'

'I'm not sure about this,' he says.

'We need that horse. Please, Joe.'

'I don't even know where it is,' Joe says.

Then, 'But maybe I can find out. I'll try, all right?'

I tell him thanks.

'You should get some kip, you look knackered,' Joe tells me, as we start back down the slope to the vans. Kip meaning sleep. Meaning shut eye. Meaning I haven't had a decent night for a week now. 'I bloody hope you're right about this fella,' he adds.

'I am,' I say.

Joe nods, but there's doubt in his face. It's still there when I look back from the square a couple of minutes later, the doubt. Joe waving back to me, as still and doubtful and beautiful as I've ever seen him.

NINETEEN

The next days have us playing nurse.

It's not as easy as you'd think. Max has a bad fever, which means he's drifting in and out of sleep, so it's impossible to be around at the right time to feed him or make sure he's drinking. And when he is awake, he's sort of delirious, not knowing what he's saying.

Joe's spooked by it at first, I see that. He stands well back in the van while I see about things – rearranging the bloke on the sofa, or trying to get him to go to the bed. Making something to eat – sarnies, pizza, anything I can sneak out of the shop without Mam or the part-time lady who mans the till noticing, which isn't much. So in the end I'm using my own money to buy stuff from the mini supermarket half a mile down the road.

'Can he tell we're here?' Joe asks, when Max is having a particularly bad time of it, thrashing about in his sleep and mumbling things. By now I've managed to wash the cuts and grazes with a wet tea towel, put on antiseptic, changed his shirt, even washed his hands, which took a while.

'Sometimes,' I say, folding a wad of kitchen roll to dry off the fella's fingers. His nails are long, black dirt under them, impossible to get out.

'What if he dies?' Joe says. 'How'll we get rid of the bugger?'

One of the things on Joe's list comes back to me: See a dead body. It's something I've been thinking about, too, of course, so I know how to answer.

'We better make sure he doesn't, eh? Either that or we call the police.'

'No police, Rabbit, please.'

We agree, but I notice how still Joe is, how quiet when he's in the van. Like he's turning into me the more time goes by. Quiet as a rabbit.

The hard thing is not letting anyone see us coming in and out of the place, especially in the daytime. But luckily there are lots of bookings this week, which means Mam is too busy to notice me heading up to forty-six every few hours. It's harder for Joe, of course, because Win or Billy's always there. But the first day goes by without much of a problem. The next morning, though, Joe texts to say he can't make it to the van. That Billy's getting suspicious about something, and Joe needs to hang around the bungalow so he doesn't make it worse. Says Billy's asking too many questions.

So I make it to Max alone, give him something to eat, make sure he's taken his paracetamol, done all that business, then it's back down the square to help my mam. Round about lunchtime, Win waves me over on her way to the beach. Says there's a bag of rubbish by her door and would I be kind enough to take it to the big bins.

'Seems to me like you two have some project on the go,' she says, all of a sudden. She's wearing her sunglasses so I can't see the look in her eyes. 'I've seen you dashing about the park the last couple of days.' Before I even try to say anything, she waves her hand, shushing me. 'I don't care if it's all above board or not, I'm just saying that whatever you boys are up to, don't let it get between you. There should be no bad blood between friends.'

'We're all right,' I say. 'Honest.' Middle of the day, and the top of my head is dead hot, and I can't tell if it's the high sun or my nerves. Because if Win has noticed what me and Joe have been doing, then maybe Billy has, too. 'How is he?' I ask then.

She stares back at me, no frown, but no smile either. Face open, sort of searching. 'Joe, you mean?' And she knows that I'm not asking if he's in a good mood or a bad mood, or whether he's had a decent breakfast this morning, but something deeper, something down to the bone. 'He has good times and bad,' she says, looking sort of thoughtful, a bit sad. 'It's not easy for him in this family, Rabbit, dear. Billy's not an easy person to have for a brother.'

'We've got a plan to get out of here, make something of ourselves,' I say then, and I don't know why I'm saying it, not sure if it's the stupidest thing I've ever said. But I believe it, and that's the main thing, isn't it?

Win smiles, nods. For all I know she thinks I'm barmy, but she just says, 'It's good to have plans. Well, let me know if I can help.' And she seems to want to leave it at that. But when I make a move to go, she adds, 'You know, if you wait until seven o'clock the sun shines right in my window, Rabbit.'

I don't have a clue what she's on about, and I'm wondering whether the heat's got to her, too. 'Dazzles real bright, so none of us can see a thing inside. Can't see a couple of lads running around the park. Can't see much. So maybe you and Joe should wait until seven before you start gadding about, eh?' she says. 'Whatever this project is. Best wait until then.'

TWENTY

I SEE NOTHING of Billy that afternoon, but sure enough, a couple of his mates appear around four o'clock, like they're casing the place. Just sitting around near the kiddies' playground, making sure I see them.

I feel a tension as each hour passes, like something's going to kick off. I watch them roam around the park, joking to each other, and staring in the windows of the vans they pass. There are times I'm sure they've worked out what's happening, and they're just biding their time before dragging Max out of number forty-six and piling into the pickup. Billy's not daft, after all. And he can read Joe pretty well, see his fear.

So I'm not surprised when Joe doesn't appear at the cliff before tea, like we'd arranged. That's the deal when we're supposed to be seeing Max together – Joe and me meet up at the spur, and then we make our way round the back of the vans to forty-six.

I'm waiting there when I feel someone arrive behind me. A wave of relief rushes through me, and I'm ready to smile, thinking it's Joe. But it's not Joe staring back at me. It's Billy, stinking of fags.

He stretches, yawns, like he's just got up, like he's had a nice easy day and this is all casual – him and me on the cliff, meeting like this. He doesn't say anything. He's in a T-shirt and jeans. I can see the tattoos on his arms as he reaches for another fag and lights it. A performance, all of it, wanting me to see how relaxed he is about this whole thing, making me wait until he speaks. He blows out the smoke and scratches his head with his fingers. This goes on for another few seconds, then he glances at me through half-shut eyes, screwed up with sleep.

'Joe's been busy,' he says, innocent as you like. When I don't reply, he adds: 'In case you were wondering, he's been doing stuff for me today. You don't mind, do you?'

It's one of those questions you can't answer right, whatever you say. Sort of questions bullies always ask. They don't care what the answer is, of course, they just want to make you worry about what to say back, fret. Me, I usually play the mute card, say nothing. Billy's used to it. Must think I'm the quietest lad he's ever met.

'Anyway,' Billy says, looking at his cigarette instead of at me. 'Just thought I'd tell you, in case you've been looking for him. Costs nothing to be polite, eh?' He's turning, like that's it, and he's off now, thanks for the natter. I believe it for a second, until he stops and looks back at me and says, 'You're a bit of nosy sod, right? I mean, you've got a good idea who comes and goes around here, haven't you?'

I shrug. It's the most I've moved since Billy arrived. That's what he does to you – makes you not want to even blink, in case it sets him off. Like a rabbit when it sees a fox. Because he's got a short fuse, has Billy, and any wrong word or movement seems to get him going.

'You don't happen to have seen anyone strange round here lately?' he asks.

'Just tourists,' I say, keeping my voice blank, unreadable.

Billy nods, acts all grown-up and calm. He stares down at his boots. 'You and me have always got on, haven't we? I mean, we don't have any bother, do we?'

'Suppose.'

'I'd like to leave it that way.' He steps up close to me, so close I can smell the dry stink of tobacco on his breath. He's tall, is Billy, and he looms over me, bends his head down until his chin is almost touching my temple. He talks really quiet when he says, 'Any friend of our lad is a mate of mine, yeah? Better than a mate. You're almost part of the family, Rabbit. You could be my little brother. And families help each other out, right? *Right?*' he repeats, when I don't answer.

I nod, look up long enough to see his grey eyes staring down at me.

'He's a ratty little fella. Pair of glasses on him. Short,' he says, 'like you.' He waits, like he wants me to say something, or maybe he's just looking for a reaction. 'I've got something he wants. So if you do see anyone looks like that, you'll come to me, won't you?' He's holding the hand with the cigarette in front of his chest and, as he talks, he raises it so it's by my left ear. I hear the tip sizzle and burn in the air. 'Won't you, Rabbit?'

'Course,' I say, trying not to shake.

'That's a promise, then.'

I feel the heat of the fag end close to my cheek, and all the while Billy holds his face so near to mine that I think I'm never going to be free of him. That I've forgotten what it's like not to be lost in his stink.

'Good lad,' he says, and suddenly he steps back. Next moment, I'm watching him stride down the bank, back towards Win's bungalow. 'I always like talking to you, Rabbit,' he says, across his shoulder. 'You listen.' He turns on his heels, spins around, like he's performing a little dance, throws his arms out wide and grins. 'If Joe can learn from you, maybe I won't have to be so hard on the little bastard in future.' A wider grin now, mean, cold. 'Oh, and remember that promise,' he adds, pointing at me. Then he flicks his fag end into the grass as he turns back home. 'People who break their promises to me don't end up too happy.'

The night goes by without any more drama, and the next morning Joe's at the spur when I arrive. It looks like things are turning up. Max is strong enough to go get a shower now, which we're all glad about, because the van stinks like a rugby team's spent a week in there, and another day of him lying in his own reek and I thought we'd have to fumigate the place.

'Soon as I get my horse I'll be out of your hair,' Max says, when he comes out of the shower. 'Won't be long.' He's wrapped in a towel, but it's not big enough to hide the horrid bruises over his chest and on his side, plum-dark and spreading from his spine to his navel. I notice Joe turn away, like he can't look. 'I don't suppose either of you have heard anything about Billy? What he's up to? I could do with getting my mobile back.'

He's looking at Joe when he says it, because, you see, I've already told him Joe is Billy's brother. Only thing is, I haven't let on to Joe that he knows, so Joe's looking at me now with thunder in his eyes.

'You told him?' Joe says. He doesn't like being here with Max, hasn't from the start, and now he looks like he'd rather be anywhere else but in the caravan.

While I'm still struggling to answer, Max drags on some jeans, says, 'Billy's your brother, right?'

'He's our lad, yeah,' Joe replies, fronting up a bit. 'What of it?'

Our lad meaning brother, meaning family, meaning not to mess

116

with the Fluddes if you've got any sense. And I know Joe hates Billy, but listening to him right now you'd think they were best mates, and that Joe's proud to be Billy's little brother. Which goes to show that families don't make a lot of sense.

Max just nods, and I admire him even more for it. Because there's no anger there, he just nods, and some of that front in Joe melts a bit. 'OK,' he says. 'I'd like your help, if you think you can.'

A moment passes. A silent moment, heavy with tension. 'I can have a look about the bungalow, if you like,' Joe says, his voice softer now. 'But I can't promise anything.'

'I'd appreciate that,' Max says, nodding to himself. 'Thank you, Joe.'

TWENTY-ONE

It's on Friday morning we hear about the horse. Not even a week's passed since I saw the hole for the first time.

There's already a text when I wake. From Joe: *I've seen her! Be at the gate at 9.*

So I've had a shower and I've dressed, and now I'm itching to get going. Find the horse and then maybe all this can go away – and the dreams with it. Because it's five to the hour, and time to meet Joe, time to move. But today of all days, Mam's decided to have a home morning. Her and me, and lots of heart-to-hearts, I'm thinking. Lots of questions about Joe and what's going on between us, and why I'm not sleeping.

'Everything OK between you two?' she asks. 'Are you fighting?'

Thing is, me and Joe have been so busy taking turns with Max, and making sure no one sees us, that we've hardly spent time together the last few days, and Mam's noticed.

'We're OK, yeah,' I say. I'm standing there trying to not look too panicky, too eager to go, because she's worried about me, I see that. And I've put Mam through enough over the years without making her worry more. 'He's been busy with Billy, that's all,' I add. 'But I'm just off to see him now, spend the day out.'

'Oh well, that's good.' Her face brightens, looks more like the Mam before. The happy Mam. We're in the kitchen, Mam having a glass of water while the dishwasher starts.

'You all right?' I ask, and the thing is no one hardly ever asks my mam how she is – she's the one does the asking – so a real tender look comes over her face. She drags the hair from her forehead, and it looks like she might actually cry, and suddenly I'm feeling bad, because I didn't want to make her cry. 'Mam?'

'I'm just being silly,' she says. And she looks at me, full in the face. 'Yes, I'm fine, love.' She does this thing with her shoulders – draws them back and puts her chin up, like she's preparing for a hike or something. Sniffs. 'Once I've got these vans cleaned and changed, I will be anyway. Oh, and the police called this morning, just to say we might see more of them in the next week or so. Says they're stepping up patrols, because of this arsonist. So if we see them, not to worry.'

But I am worrying, because it's hard enough sneaking about the place without Billy getting suspicious, let alone the coppers.

'Here, does that mean there've been more fires?' I ask, trying to sound casual.

I'm leaning against the wall, my hands behind my back. Standing in a hot square of sunlight coming through the window.

'You mean farm fires? Not recently, why?'

It makes sense, I'm thinking. Billy's too busy looking for Max and worrying he might have gone to the coppers to be carrying on with the farms. 'Just wondering. You know, with the coppers getting in touch.'

'No, they didn't say,' she says. 'Are you worried about the fires?'

'Just funny how they haven't caught anyone yet.'

'Has Joe said something about them?' Mam's suspicions are coming back like a wave on the tide. She's looking at me over the rim of the glass. Her face all kind, but watchful.

'Him? Joe knows less about them than me.' Another lie. It eats away at me, I feel it in my chest.

'And Billy?'

I flinch. 'What about Billy?'

'Well, he's always close to trouble, isn't he? Haven't you ever wondered if he knows something about it all?'

There's a lot I know now about Billy, but I can't tell Mam, no matter how much I'd like to. Mam would see things right, if she could, I know that. She'd get the cops involved, social services, but then where would Joe be? Anyway, no one can control Billy, and if the cops decided *not* to do anything it would just get Joe into more bother, more hidings. Maybe dead, like he says.

But part of me wants to tell her. A big part wants this to be over one way or another, and soon. You better believe it.

'If it is Billy behind them, what will the cops do to him? Will he go to prison?' I say, and I'm feeling myself get all worried again, like I'm about to blush. I fight it, make myself stand still, calm. Like Dad. Like a rock, because that's what I'd like to be. Just steady and unshakeable so I'll never blush again, never be frightened. Mam must see it cross my face, the memory of Dad, because she says:

120

'Have you been thinking about him a lot? Your dad?'

It's like I'm made of glass, like I'm see-through, like every bloody thought I have is all over my face. I don't nod but by my silence she knows she's right.

The bloke in the hole, something about him – ever since we saw him down there my mind's been going back to living in the woods, me and Dad. That time together. And him needing me. Me letting him down.

'You look tired. You haven't been having dreams again?' she asks, and that look comes on her face that always makes me feel bad. This real loving look, but sad, pitying, scared. 'Maybe I'll call Louise today, see if she's free.'

'No—' I say. I smile, trying to hide the panic I'm feeling, but my face isn't up to smiling right now. 'No dreams. It's just hot, isn't it? Makes it hard to sleep.'

Mam nods, but the worry's still there.

'He'd be proud, you know,' she says. 'Of you.' And that's all she has to say and there's a pressure behind my eyes now, proper heavy weight that makes my head ring. Because she doesn't know what stupid game I've got myself caught up in, helping some bloke I don't know from Adam.

I feel the tears well up, and I fight them back, because I've had enough of crying. And anyway, she's wrong. He wouldn't be proud of me. He'd call me a silly sod for getting involved with something I had no right to mess with, because now I've brought the danger here, to my mam, to my home.

121

I rub my face, breathe. Let out one deep sigh, and Mam's here giving me a hug and telling me she loves me. Which just makes everything seem ten times worse.

It feels like she'll never let me go, when I hear Joe's voice. We turn to see him at the door, framed in the sunlight. And by the look on his face I know he's up to something, trying to help me out. 'Nan says you're invited round for a coffee,' he tells my mam, his eyes shifting briefly to me, to my face, seeing the wet in my eyes. 'Is it a bad time?'

'No, Joe, it's OK. Tell her I'll be there in a sec,' Mam says. She squeezes my arms, stares into my face, nods, as if to say, *Everything's all right*. And then all three of us are out in the square, heading to Win's place, and Joe giving me a wink behind Mam's back.

Talking himself out of trouble, out of the grave. Like always.

TWENTY-TWO

So HERE'S THE story Joe tells me: Billy and him went up the coast first thing, before it was even light. They were buying up some old gas tanks, and the last place they ended up just happened to have a horse there. White horse, like the one Joe had seen that night in the field. Max's horse. At least that's what I think he says, because Joe tells me all this in a rush, as me and him make our way around the back of the vans. The one thing I haven't thought about is how we get to wherever we're going, wherever the horse is being held. But when we arrive at the main gate of the park, there's an old dirt bike parked up that looks like it was last ridden back when my dad was a nipper.

'Well,' Joe says, walking up to it and grabbing the handles and kicking away the side stand. 'No point us walking there. We'd arrive next week.'

'Where is it we're going exactly?'

'Not far,' he says, 'but it's quicker on this thing.'

'Was she all right when you saw her? The horse?'

'She's standing, if that's what you mean,' Joe says. 'Billy didn't want us hanging around there long, so I didn't get much of a look. Well, are you getting on?'

I'm still peering at the bike, noticing the rust and the muck. 'Can you ride it?'

Joe grins. 'Course,' he says. 'Been riding these things as long as I've been riding horses.' He looks at me and winks.

Shit, I'm thinking, because I don't believe Joe can ride a horse any more than I believe he can find spring water.

'We old enough?' I ask, trying to sow some doubt into his mind – enough doubt to stop him from killing us both.

Joe turns the key, sits astride the bike and guns the engine. It roars loud enough for Mam to hear it back at the square. Real rough dirty sound like the engine's about to die and this is its last party. Joe cups his ear, still grinning. 'Eh?' he yells. He's laughing. Carefree Joe back, for now. Because soon we'll be free of the horse and free of Max, and everything will be sweet again, is what he's thinking. He jabs his head sideways, encouraging me to climb behind him.

I just wait there, feel the thrumming of the engine in the soles of my trainers. If Mam sees me getting on Joe's bike, she'll kill me before he can, I'm thinking.

He looks at me and furrows his brow. I read his lips, because there's no way I can hear him over the din: *What's up?*

I shake my head.

Joe turns off the engine. The noise cuts out. Just the summer sky hissing with heat now. Birds calling somewhere.

'What is it? It's not nicked, if that's what you're thinking. It's my cousin's bike.'

'I'm just not a fan,' I say. That pattering feeling in my chest. Adrenalin in my blood.

Joe gets it, just like that. 'Your dad?' he asks.

See, last time I was near a bike it was the day my dad died. I can still see him revving the thing in a quarry at the edge of the woods where he was killed only a few minutes later. His eyes bright and heavy, face only half visible in the helmet, before I watched him ride that thing until he couldn't go any further.

'What if we go to the coppers? Tell them about the horse, about Max,' I say.

Joe shakes his head. 'If you want me banged up, we can. Do you?'

'No, but—'

'After today it'll be over,' he says. 'Come and see for yourself – the horse isn't even chained up or anything. It'll be all right, honest,' Joe adds, when I still haven't moved. 'Trust me, yeah? Walking will take us hours.'

He holds out his hand for me to take.

'Just grab on and close your eyes.' I must look at his hand for what feels like an eternity. Then I'm on the back of the bike, arms wrapped around him. The engine starts again, and a moment later we're heading down the long straight road, into East Ferry.

TWENTY-THREE

IT's A JUNKYARD. Or it looks like, anyhow. A wide square compound surrounded by a patchwork boundary of brick wall, chain-link fence, chicken netting, barbed wire, plywood sheets and overgrown brambles – all jumbled together like the place has been here so long it needs to be patched up and rebuilt every decade or so. We're on the other side of East Ferry, about half a mile out from the harbour, the back end of town that leads up the coast. It's not all run down around here, though. There are the white sticks of the rugby ground not far away, and if you crane your neck you can see the rolling hills of a golf course, built for the tourists, sinking away to the blue band of sea. I'm guessing none of the golfers look this way while they play, though. It's a proper eyesore.

'I saw her around the corner here,' Joe explains, as we move towards the fence. 'I've been here before once or twice. The old bloke who runs it gives Billy some knock-off gear sometimes.'

In the yard, a dog is yapping on the hard, orange ground outside a breezeblock cabin that's topped with corrugated iron. Brown dog, it is, with a black zag for a mouth.

The place is full of scrap. There's a pile of old lorry tyres that stands higher than the cabin. Knackered washing machines litter the open spaces of muck and baked-down clay, about a dozen of them. And the rest of the place is cluttered with hollowed-out carcasses of cars, some of them so rusted they look like they're merging into the ground. Like the clay is slowly leeching into the metal, rotting it from the inside out and weeding it over.

'Do you know the owner, then?'

Joe shakes his head. We propped up the bike a road back, and walked the rest of the way, not wanting to be conspicuous. Now we're hiding behind a plyboard sheet about the size of a tank that's by the locked double gate.

'But this is where you saw it, yeah?'

'Billy and the geezer were in the cabin. I got as close as I could before that bloody dog started yapping.'

It's a mongrel, the dog. Some skinny thing, all ribs and snarl. Hungry dogs are the most vicious, my dad always said, and I can tell this one would have your hand off for fun. It's chained up, I can see that much from here, but it's a worryingly long chain.

Joe stops and looks at me a moment, real serious. 'Just one thing,' he says. 'I can't get her out, OK?'

'What?'

'It's best if I stay close to Billy while you and Max get her. You see that, right? I'll keep an eye on him at the park, let you know if he has plans to come back here.'

I'm about to argue, because I'd much rather he was with us. But he's right. It makes sense, what he says. Although, I can't help seeing the fear in him, too. He's scared of breaking the horse out. Scared of what Billy would do when he finds out.

'Billy makes a move, I'll warn you,' Joe says, trying to sound tough. 'But if Max wants it, he'll have to get it himself.'

And me, I nod, because I get it. I do. 'Show me,' is all I say.

So Joe walks down the line of brick, waves for me to follow. Where the brick meets a tall chain-link section, he stops, juts his chin across the way. He's being real quiet, I notice. I don't like it when Joe's quiet. It usually means there's danger about.

I follow his gaze, but there's no horse. Just a load more tyres, all set in sort of a jumbled ring. The back of a blue Portaloo. An old black bucket, half green with mould set on the ground.

'I don't see anything,' I say.

'*There*—' Joe says, more urgently.

A shadow by the bucket, then something grey dips down, and the outline of a horse's head is visible from behind a stack of wooden pallets. Grey head, rough with bristle.

'Jeez, how old is it?'

'The horse?' Joe shrugs. 'Ancient.'

It steps forward. Here's a hoof, big, sending up a thin beat of dust. The blunt head of the thing noses the bucket, then tips its chin up, like it's seen us. There's the black eye, a gleam of sun. She blinks, the horse. A bright web of lashes.

'She's on a thin rope, that's all,' Joe says. 'Tied to a head collar, see? So no bother getting her. Just make sure it's night time, dark.

No way you and Max can free her in daylight.'

The rope's not the problem, I see that much. The fence is, though. And then the skinny guard dog. And that's if whoever's in that cabin doesn't see me and shoot me for trespassing.

The horse tosses its head back, still staring at us. Taps its hoof on the ground, like it's ready to come over. Like we've got food for it. Or maybe it just wants the company. I elbow Joe away, before the nag draws attention to us.

'Come on,' I say, and we move back down the road, looking to Joe only when we get to the corner.

'Another thing,' he says. 'Good news this time.' He reaches into his jeans and then he's holding out a mobile to me. Its screen is cracked, and it looks like it's been kicked about a bit. But I know what it is, and what it means, and I want to hug Joe right then. 'Sneaked into the bastard's room when he was out,' he tells me, looking proud. 'Wasn't easy, and when he finds out, I'm a dead man.'

'You can stay at mine, live with us maybe,' I say, meaning it, because since we talked I've been thinking long and hard. 'I'll ask Mam tomorrow.'

Joe's smile isn't as wide any more. I can see he doesn't believe me. 'Anyway, I'd say we've got until the morning before he sees it's missing.'

'That's enough time,' I say, glancing to the yard, and suddenly I'm feeling hopeful.

The horse is still staring at us, its old face held high, eyes blank.

TWENTY-FOUR

'**S**HE'S ALIVE,' I say later, to Max, when I'm back at the van.

'I never doubted it. She'll live longer than me, that one.' He's lying down in the dark. Mrs Wickman's old caravan has the same set-up as most of the others – there's a long sofa that runs beneath the windows at the side, down to the patio doors. The glass doors have a view onto the sea when the curtains are open, but this afternoon the curtains are closed tight again.

Max isn't big, but he's still managing to sprawl over most of the sofa. He's had another shower, his hair still wet. His glasses set on the coffee table, the one good lens fogged. His clothes are almost as dirty as they had been down that hole, even though I've soaked them in the kitchen sink a couple of times. I see my Dad's clobber folded and back on the table where they were all those days ago. He's changed out of them.

Clobber meaning clothes. Meaning kecks and a shirt. Meaning, after today, along with his horse and his mobile, Max is on his way.

'You all right?' he says, seeing me stare at the table. 'Johnny?'

'Yeah,' I say. 'Oh, I've got this for you.' I hand him the mobile, and he pulls himself upright, sits on the edge of the sofa. 'I charged it for you.'

His eyes sort of light up. He's grinning real wide, but the grin stops when he sees the same look is still on my face. He glances to the clothes on the table. 'They're your dad's,' he says, recognising the confusion in my eyes. 'It didn't feel right wearing them, sorry. But thank you, Johnny. And for *this*,' he adds, holding up the mobile. He begins to check to see if it still works. 'How the hell did you get your hands on it?'

'Honest, really, I don't mind,' I say. 'About the clobber, I mean. Anyway, you can't go round in bloody clothes. Those stains won't come out, I've tried. People will notice.'

I carry the first aid kit from the kitchen cupboard, and I put it down on the sofa next to him, open the lid. It's our routine now, every day. He unbuttons his shirt and starts putting some antiseptic cream on his side, over the scratches and cuts, and I help with his back where he can't reach. It's bruised and raw, scabbed over in places. I can still see the deep purple imprint of Billy's boots on his ribs. Then I put on a fresh bit of gauze, and bandage it up.

'How do you know how to do this?' he asks, trying not to wince, as I pull the bandage tighter.

'Dad got in some scrapes, too,' I tell him. 'We patched him up a couple of times, me and Mam. Bit of bandage and an iodine patch does wonders.'

'What was he like, your dad?'

I'm not sure how to answer that, never have been. When he was alive he could be all sorts of different types – loving, tough, selfish, kind. Sometimes he could say the meanest things, and a moment later break down crying. 'A bit like you,' I say, in the end.

'How's that?' Max asks.

'Stubborn.'

He laughs. There are cuts on his hands. From the broken bottles in the hole, I'm thinking. But they're healing. In the last couple of days, one of his eyes has gone from brown to black to this odd shade of greenish yellow. I'm OK with this sort of stuff, it doesn't bother me. Only, every time I'm here, each time I see Max's injuries, I start thinking of Joe, and what he must have put up with all these years from Billy.

'Someone's got to do for him one day,' I say. I'm assuming Max is thinking about Billy, too, because he's looking thoughtful and a bit sad.

But then he says, 'It sounds like you've had a tough life.'

And I realise the sadness is for me. I hear some of that pity in his voice, too, but I ignore it. I'm not a pity case, never have been. And Dad would never have stood for sympathy.

'It's not far to your horse,' I say, changing the subject. 'I can take you there tonight.'

I watch as Max thinks things over. Making little calculations. His body's short and thick, but there's no fat on him. Not as strong as my dad, but maybe the time down the hole and the days in here have made him lose muscle. He's slow standing up, and twitchy, like he's full of nerves. Sucking in air between his teeth, trying to ignore the pain, because the ribs are nowhere near healing yet. 'How far is it?'

'We can walk it in an hour or so.'

Actually, it'll take longer than that, but I don't want to put him off or delay him. I want him out tonight, if possible, and no fuss.

'Where?'

'Junkyard other side of town.'

'How'd you find it?'

'I didn't. Joe did.'

'Close, you two, aren't you?' He drags his fingers through his hair, rubs at it like he's still not used to the clean feeling. 'You a couple?'

'It's not like that,' I say, too quick.

'It's fine if you are,' he says. 'There's nothing to be ashamed about loving someone.' And I almost believe him, but not quite. Because, the thing is you can't tell anyone about love. Not in East Ferry, not with how they think. How do you say you love a lad to them? Maybe if I were stronger, braver. And what Mam says about Dad being proud of me comes back, and feels like those nettle stings are all over me again, because no way would he have put up with me being too scared to admit love. Love was all there was, he'd say. Love and nothing else.

'We're just mates.'

'Mates like you two are rare.' Max isn't quite smiling, but there's a look in his face, something warm. 'I've seen you two argue and I've seen you fight, then the next minute it's all blown over. It's good. And the way you two have looked after me – well, I just wanted to say thank you. To Joe, too.' There's a different sort of sadness there now, the sort I can't read. It's almost like he's going to be unhappy to leave, I'm thinking. Like this has been a holiday or something.

'You'll be out of here soon,' I say, trying to encourage him.

'And what about you two?' he says.

'What about us?'

135

'Like you say, someone needs to take Billy down, don't they? This place,' he nods to the van, but he means more than that. He means the park, Mam and Win, all of it. 'It's a real home, isn't it? Or could be. Billy's the only one standing in the way.' He's glancing at the mobile as it starts up, sort of eager. And I get the feeling he's planning something, but I've no idea what, and part of me doesn't want to know. Because it feels like it won't be long till he's away with his horse, and then maybe life can get back to normal, and anything new will scupper it all probably. 'Maybe there's a way to get him out of your lives for good,' he says. 'Get him banged up.'

'If we get the coppers involved, they'll lock up Joe, too. And what good will that do?'

'You sure of that? Because I'm not.'

I shrug. 'It's not worth the risk.' Before he can start up the conversation again, I ask, 'So what's *your* dad like? You two close?'

I start packing away the first aid kit. Max helps, putting the top on the cream, rolling up the bandage. I can see he wants to carry on the talk about the coppers, but he says, 'I haven't seen him for a while.'

'How come?'

'When my old man found out I was leaving to find work, he wasn't happy.'

'Was this the circus?'

'Yeah, he didn't think it was a real job, still doesn't.' He wipes his palms on his sides, picks up the mobile, checks something on it, then puts it in his pocket.

It's hot in here, and the air is still humid from the shower, thick with sweat and the smell of antiseptic. 'My old man's an angry fella, Johnny. I don't mind anger, though. Anger's good,' he says. 'Anger's righteous. Plenty to be angry about in this world, that's what I say.' He looks at me.

'Now you sound like my dad,' I say. And he does, too.

'You must miss him.'

I don't need to answer, and he sees as much. 'Use that anger, kid. Can be a good friend to you.'

And what if that anger is aimed at a man who's dead, I want to say. What if the person you're really angry at isn't here any more. Because, Dad, he should be here. He should never have got himself killed. He should be alive and living with me and Mam—

'Here,' I say, handing him my Dad's top. 'Take it. I want you to have it.'

He hesitates, but then takes off his shirt and puts it on. It fits him, almost.

'He was your hero, wasn't he?' Max says, admiring himself.

'Sort of.'

'How did he die? You never said.'

I don't say anything for a bit, and he adds, very gently, 'God, he didn't top himself, did he?'

Top himself, meaning suicide.

I shake my head and wait a second before answering. 'He was shot.'

TWENTY-FIVE

Max DOESN'T HIDE his surprise. He's sitting down, hands together between his knees, just listening.

'He got in with some bad men back where I used to live,' I continue.

'And they shot him? The bad men?'

'No,' I say. And, funnily enough, my voice is quite steady. You'd think this would be the time for me to fall apart and cry and stuff. But whenever I talk about Dad, I feel calm somehow. Like he's here with me, holding me still. 'He had mental problems, they said. And he went to live in the woods, and I went with him for a bit, because he couldn't do with people any more and I went to look after him. Anyway, he got in with these men, like gangsters, and he stole some money, and the cops arrived, and Dad, he just stayed there in the trees and wouldn't come out. He was in a bad way. He had this shotgun.'

Max says nothing. Waits, gentle and calm. Dad would have liked him, because he didn't like noisy men, blokes with plenty to say for themselves.

'I should have stopped him, because I knew he wasn't right. So it was my fault really.'

Max is going to say something – tell me it wasn't my fault, of course, and what could I have done. But before he does, I say, 'The police shot him in the end, said he was a danger to people. And the truth is, they were right. He was a danger, especially to himself.' I'm breathing harder now, but I manage to add, 'Not much of a hero then, was he? Not really.'

Max looks pale. Maybe he was thinking my dad died because of cancer or a road accident, not a shoot-out with the cops. Which is one of the reasons why I never tell anyone. Why I'm quiet as a rabbit, because it's not something you boast about, is it? That your dad was a criminal, that he got killed for no reason. 'Well, I can see why you don't want to go to the cops,' he says. 'Don't think I would either if they did for my old man. But there are different sorts of heroes,' Max says then, his voice calm and steady. 'We all need one.'

Now, seeing the tender look on his face, that's when I feel myself welling up, and I make sure to swallow down the feeling, because I don't want him seeing me cry.

'Keep hold of your heroes, Johnny,' Max continues, and his hand is on my shoulder. He looks like he's about to offer some words of comfort, but stops himself, like he knows I must have heard them all.

My voice breaks a bit when I speak again. 'The junkyard is guarded,' I say, trying to pull myself together. 'There's a fence, a gate. Some mangy dog wandering the place.'

Max takes it in. Knows to move on. 'OK,' he says and nods to himself. 'I suppose your mother has tools around here? Bolt cutters? Can you get them?'

I tell him I can.

'And something heavy. A spanner or a hammer. We'll go tonight. Midnight, if we can. Then you two will be free of me.' He looks at me, frowns. 'Bring Joe if you need to.'

'He'll stay here, keep an eye on Billy.'

Max doesn't argue. 'Good idea. Oh, we'll want a rope.'

'Already has one,' I say. 'The horse, I mean. She's tied up, still has her head collar on.' I'm about to go, leave him to his planning. And then something comes to me, something that's been on my mind. 'Here, I've got a question for you.'

'Go on.'

'How'd you get out?' I ask. 'From the hole?'

Max looks at me, more surprise in his face. He shrugs. 'You left the cable hanging down, and the rock under the door.'

'No offence, but until today you could hardly walk straight,' I say. 'So how did you climb out of a hole that deep?'

His mind's elsewhere, I see that. But then what I'm saying clicks, and he stares at me. 'Well, you can do a lot when you need to. More than you ever imagine. You know that.' The way he looks at me, it's like he knows me somehow, can see into me like Mam can see into me. 'Sometimes, you're much stronger than you think you are, aren't you?'

'I suppose.'

A smile comes to his face. 'Anyway, I always knew I'd get out of there. I dreamed about it. Two days, I spent in that hole, and the second night, I dreamed I was climbing out.

Funny things, dreams. Sometimes you dream something and then it arrives, like magic. You ever had that?'

I keep my mouth shut. I haven't mentioned the dreams of wolves or the horse, and I've no intention to. I've already said enough.

'Well, that's what happened with me and you,' Max says. 'I dreamed you'd come and you did, just like that.' He gives me one last grin, as we cross to the patio doors. 'I think maybe I *dreamed* you up to save me, Johnny Hill.'

PART THREE

TWENTY-SIX

W<small>E'RE MADE OF</small> stars. That's what they say.

When this universe cracked open and all the stars spilled out, burning up over time, they released atoms, shot them out all over like glitter, hotter than lava. And all these atoms and elements drifted out further and further and became us. All the calcium in our bones and iron in our blood comes from a star. At least, that's what Sophie told me, and my dad thought the same. Stars were Sophie's thing. She told me that whenever I felt scared I should think about how everything is connected, everything that's alive or ever was alive, everything dead, everything that ever shined or burned or sparked with life is in us now and around us, and for ever. That meant me and her were connected, no matter where we were, she said. Me and Dad, too. Me and everything in the universe. All of it is one and together, held together with a love like atoms.

I tell myself this in the night, when I wake up sweating. I check the clock: *11:22 p.m.* Good time, I think, and at least I got some kip. I hold myself still in my damp bed, breathe in the warm air of my bedroom and I picture all that blackness out there, and those dim little gleams of light shining, and I think of me and Dad, and me and Sophie. I think of Mam asleep in the other room, and how Dad's in me and he's in her, too. How maybe she dreams of him, like I do. I think of space and the blackness there, and the dark leads me into the hole in the field, and the shining specs of the bloke called Max. The smell of that pit they slung him in.

Then it's the horse in my head again.

It's out there in the high waves, night water crashing about its wild eyes. It's swimming, or trying to. The ghost of a horse struggling to keep its head up. And me, I'm trying to encourage it back to shore, but it won't come. So now I'm wading out there, in the cold and dark, trying to get to it before it sinks. Which is dead stupid, I know, because what am I going to do when I get to it? Me against some great lump of a horse? But there I am, swimming now. Getting closer, wary of its thrashing hooves. Then my arms are around its neck, and I'm climbing across its back, and I'm gasping for air. And you can bet I'm thinking of that kelpie Joe told me about, how it lures you in to drown you. But right now this horse looks scared to death.

'I'm here,' I say to her. And then louder: 'I'm here.' Like it might calm her. Like my voice in her ear will soothe the storm in her heart, big as a football. 'I'm here, girl.'

For a moment, it seems to work. I feel her begin to slow. Her great white legs stop thrashing, and her eye doesn't flicker so wide any more. We move through the water nice and steady, me and her. And after a minute, I'm thinking we'll be OK. This is no kelpie, just a horse that needs rescuing. Everything will be OK, we just have to make it back to the shore now.

I see it then.

The shoreline.

And I see what the horse has been so scared of all this time.

It's on fire. The whole shoreline is orange with flame, smoke billowing into the sky. Just a thick band of orange fire that follows the horizon as far as I can see. And I realise there's no way back. Because there is no 'back' to get to. The land is aflame.

When I wake the second time, I'm kicking. My chest is wet with sweat and my arms ache like I've been fighting in my sleep. Not fighting, I tell myself, but swimming. Swimming in my sleep. Me and Max's horse.

It's twenty minutes past midnight now. I'm late.

Shit.

And, while I rush to put on my jeans, I'm thinking that it doesn't matter where the calcium in my bones comes from, doesn't matter about the iron in my blood. All that matters is the pain, because pain's all the same. And I bet that horse out there, stuck in the yard, she won't be worrying about the universe or the stars. She just wants out, that's all. Waiting for us. Me and Max. And if I want to help her then I need to clear my head, and make sure none of us gets killed along the way.

TWENTY-SEVEN

By the way, heroes aren't born. That's what Dad told me, and he'd known a few, he said.

'They're not born, they're made,' he'd say. And he didn't mean, folk grew to be heroes. He meant they were made, like a story is made-up. Like, it's not real. 'Every hero I've known has been a let-down,' he said. 'It's not their fault. It's us that bring them down, because we expect them to be better than us, to be stronger or braver or more clever. And in the end, they're just like us, no better or worse.' Which makes him sound like a right misery guts, but he wasn't.

So Max is wrong, see. I've no illusions about heroes. I know I'm not one, and never will be. I'm scared. Always have been. Although, Dad said that's what makes courage, because courage without fear is just recklessness. Without fear there are no heroes, only zealots.

And so, by rights, that must make me the bravest fella on earth, because I'm always scared. Scared of letting people down. Scared of what I don't know. Scared my dreams will come back. Scared I'll stop talking. Only time I wasn't scared was with Joe, because he was a hero to me, too. And, yeah, I know they don't exist, not really. But if they did, Joe was as close as you could get. Before. Because there wasn't much that seemed to bother him, or make him question himself, or that's what I thought. He had this confidence that was beautiful and hot as sunshine. Except, of course, for one thing. One thing undermined it all. Because, yeah, Joe could talk his way out of trouble, like he said. Like a magic trick.

But the only one his magic didn't work on was Billy.

Billy was the hole in Joe's chest, this wound that wouldn't close.

And the thing is, I never knew how deep it went, until now.

'I thought you weren't coming,' Max says, once I'm at the van. 'Thought you'd lost your nerve.'

We're outside the van, round the back so no one will see. Max's face is wet with sweat, like he's been sat here in a panic. Or maybe it's excitement, I can't tell. 'I want to show you something,' he says, fishing in his pocket. 'Here—'

'You're not taking anything?' I say, not listening to him. I'm worried. I'm expecting him to bring some of the food or clothes. Ready to sling his hook, once the horse is free.

'What have I to bring?' he says, and maybe he's not thinking straight, or maybe the plan has changed without me knowing. I'm about to ask him whether he's heading off tonight or not, when he says, 'Watch this.'

He's holding his mobile out to me, showing me a video or something. I'm wondering what the bloody hell, because here we are, about to break a horse out and risk our necks doing it, and he's showing me funny videos.

Only, the video, it isn't funny. It's dark and shaky, and I don't have a clue what I'm looking at, until I hear Billy's voice. And then I see the flames. 'What is it?' I say.

'Proof,' Max tells me. 'Shut up and watch.'

It's a video of Billy and his mates. Billy has a load of rags in his hand, and he's lit them. Now he's walking to the edge of a shed, and throwing the bundle of rags on the ground. And as he does it, he turns to the camera and yells something, swears, then gives a big grin. A moment later the fire spreads through the shed, and then the flames climb up the walls.

Max turns it off, pockets it. He looks at me. 'You got the tools, right?'

'Bollocks,' I say. 'Sorry.' I've been so busy trying not to make Mam suspicious, I'd forgotten all about the tools.

He grabs the bag off me, looks inside. Sees the bottle of water I brought, and no sign of any bolt cutters, no spanner. 'You joking?' he says, and there's a spark of anger in his face. A small flame of it. He's wearing my dad's jeans and top, and if you squint, it could be him, here, now. And it could be Dad and me in the night, heading out on another adventure, and the expression on his face too serious to be safe.

My head's still reeling from the video. 'What do you mean, proof?' I say.

But Max is distracted, thinking about the tools. He isn't listening. And

I can't read him tonight, but I feel the energy in him. It feels dangerous.

'I-I know where the tools are kept,' I say, getting his attention at last. I take him to the maintenance shed up past the kiddies' playground, up on the brow of the cliff. It's secured with a padlock, and I watch as he finds a rock and starts to clatter at it. Noise ringing out in all directions, clear as a bloody church bell, and he doesn't seem to care. Maybe he's more scared than I thought, or maybe he's just not thinking.

'Stop,' I say, after he's given the clasp another half-dozen clouts. There's a spade leaning against the water butt, and I get it and aim a good blow with the blade at the edge of the padlock. I wait a second before doing it again, harder this time. And just like that the lock clasp comes off, and then Max is in there, searching for anything that might help us. After a couple of minutes, scrambling in the dark, the best he can come up with is a pair of long-handle edging shears, and a lump hammer I never even knew was there.

And then we're heading to the cliff path.

There are two ways to town from Happy Sands. One is going by the road, across the two-lane bridge, past the houses and bed and breakfasts where there are plenty of people to see you, and traffic to avoid. And the other is the quiet way, quicker, too, by foot – along the coastal footpath, this zigzagging of duckboards that snakes along the edge of the eroding cliffs. Thing is, the path gives way here and there where the soil's fallen into the sea. Not been used as an official public footpath since Easter, the path. Hazard tape flapping at both ends.

Can be dangerous, if you don't know it. Especially at night.

You walk so far and suddenly you see the duckboard vanish, and the barbed-wire fence trails off into thin air. More than once, me and Joe have nearly toppled down those scattering banks of soil.

But, tonight, Max walks like he's not afraid of gravity, not afraid of the rocks below. Or the noise of the sea. He walks like he knows exactly where he's going, which he doesn't, because every now and then his boots slip on the leaning duckboard, and then he's holding onto the fence, until he gets his balance back. And the thing is, he's limping a bit, but he doesn't seem to feel the pain tonight. So maybe what he says is right – maybe you can do impossible things when you need to.

'The video,' I say. 'What are you going to do with it?'

'What do you think?' he says. 'Like I say, it's proof. Soon as the coppers see it, Billy gets put away, no problem.'

'You can't,' I argue. 'What about Joe?'

Max looks sideways at me. His face is blue with moonlight, glasses shining. 'I've watched through the whole thing, and Joe's not on it. Trust me. It's just Billy and his mates. Anyway, there's no way they'd prosecute Joe. He's a kid. Anyone with sense knows Billy forced him.'

'Max, please,' I say, and I grab his arm.

He turns to me. No sign of anger now, only this quiet determination. 'I know you're scared of the coppers, Johnny, and I know why. But trust me, it's the only way to get rid of Billy and keep Joe safe.'

Funny thing is, part of me wants to tell him where to go, and part of me admires him. Maybe another part wants to be him, I'm thinking. Because there's a courage in Max tonight I haven't seen before. It's a courage I haven't got, and never had.

I fall behind him as he walks on, and I just stare. It could be Dad, I tell myself, before the bad men got to him, before the coppers in the woods. Marching out into the world, ready to take on another fight. Because there was always a fight in him. Like every day was a new struggle.

Another few metres, along the ragged line of fencing and wire.

And then I do see him – Dad, not Max. He's there, sharp as moonlight. Walking on ahead of me, big as life. My dad, walking under the stars, and any moment it's as though he might just turn and glance at me.

'Johnny?'

Dad, like before. Alive and here.

'Johnny, just stop!'

Max stares at me now, his face blank with shock. The sound of the sea beneath us, and the endless sky overhead, and I've stopped on the cliff like he told me. Stopped and I'm looking to where I just saw my dad, just now. So close I could have touched him.

'Steady,' Max says, stepping towards me and moving his arm around my shoulder, real slow. We're close to the edge, see, and he's guiding me away. I hadn't seen how close. No fence here, just muck and blackness sliding down to the sea, and the breeze tugging at my jeans, and another step and I'd have been over.

'What did you see?' he says, looking about him. Maybe he thinks the cops are here, or Billy and his mates. And how can I tell him I just saw the ghost of my old man?

'Nothing,' I say. 'It's nothing.'

But Max isn't stupid. There's something in my face that he recognises. 'It's all right,' he says. 'The night can play tricks on you, can't it? Easy to lose your way if you're not careful, so maybe we walk together, OK? Side by side, you and me?'

For the rest of the way my head is still with my dad, in the woods, and Max knows it, so he starts talking to me. Just chitchat, really, to distract my mind, I suppose. He's nice enough, I'm thinking. No edge to him, nothing bitter or bad-tempered, and it's like he's never had a hardship or worry – and I know he has, because I've looked after him these past few days, and heard him grunt every time he tries to move that battered body of his.

He asks about Mam and what it's like living on the park, and I ask

154

him about the circus, about some of the jobs he did, and he says how at the circus you get roped in to do all sorts of things, which is why he likes it. You learn, and he likes learning. So, he tells me, he didn't just ride horses, he welcomed the punters in, too, putting on a real show for them. Lots of jokes and handshakes.

Punters meaning customers. Meaning the general public. Meaning putting on a smile and trying to make them think they've come to some sort of paradise, and forget about the outside world for an hour.

'Oh, and magic,' he says. 'We'd do some magic.' And straight off, I'm thinking of the magic my dad would talk about. The magic in the night and in the trees – how the very fact that we're alive is a miracle, and how we have to protect the world from our own base instincts. Because that's how he talked about things, Dad.

But, of course, Max doesn't mean that sort of magic, but tricks. Bits of paper in your hand that would catch fire and make people jump or laugh, or how he'd make a coin disappear, then reappear out of some kid's nose.

So, I say, 'I was right about you – you are The Great Maximo!' And we both laugh at that. Then, after a bit, I ask him, 'Why does she mean so much to you, this horse?'

What I mean is, is his horse worth dying for, because that's what'll happen if he isn't careful.

'I grew up with horses on a farm. I don't know,' he says, but even as he's saying it, a smile comes on his face. 'I've ridden a few, but this one is different, she's sort of *magical*.'

That word again.

'Like how?'

'With some animals, it's like they know your thoughts. Well, she knows mine, or seems to. Soon as I got on her back, her and me just worked. You ever had that?' he asks.

I want to say I have. Because I had a dog once, with Dad in the woods. She was called Mol, and I loved her. She got me like Joe gets me, like Sophie got me. So yeah, I know the feeling all right.

'Half Moon is more than a horse, see,' Max says. 'And no way can I leave her with a bloke like Billy.'

The time goes real quick, and before we know it, we're in East Ferry. Then it's across the bridge, and there we are down the main street, with Max carrying the shears over his shoulder and the hammer tucked into his waist, and if the coppers are around, he's banged up for sure, because he looks just like a bloke about to break into someplace. But he doesn't seem to care about that, either.

'Where now?' he asks, when we get past the town centre. There are a few groups of people walking home from wherever they've been, all swaying and drunk, laughter and giggles and folk swearing. Some of them look at us funny as we pass by, but most are in their own worlds. So I take him on, down to the rugby ground, and soon enough we're there. At the junkyard. With the horse waiting, as if this was all meant to be somehow. Fate. She's white as a ghost, and her head held high, like before. Hardly changed. Staring at us, patient, eyes black and still.

Like she knew we were coming.

TWENTY-EIGHT

'GOOD GIRL,' MAX says, next to me, under his breath. We're too far away for her to hear, I'm thinking. But I see her ears twitch. 'Good girl,' he repeats. And then he says something I don't understand.

'Meia-lua.'

'What?'

'It's Portuguese,' he says, staring up at the fence. We're at the corner of the yard, as far from the breezeblock cabin as we can get and still see the horse. 'It means half moon.'

Meia-lua – I realise I've heard it before. Max had said it over and over in his sleep, but I'd just imagined it was nonsense, more of his fever talk.

'Is that her name?' I ask.

Max nods, but he's not listening now. He's reaching up to the fence, poking his fingers through, trying to test its strength. Here the fence is chain-link, but the sections are leaning badly, held together with plastic ties. There are gaps in it that have been filled with rusted chickenwire tacked against timber struts. Max kicks a foot against the nearest strut and it wobbles, like it's barely buried. Then just like that, he's cut the ties and he's pulling the chain-link section to one side, and getting me to help. A minute after ripping out the struts he hacks away with the shears at the knackered old chicken wire. The blades of the shears are blunt, but the chickenwire gives anyway, it's that rotten. And now there's a gap in the fence big enough for one of us to squeeze through if we wanted to. Except, Max has forgotten one thing.

The dog.

The nasty bleeder's there, all right.

Thing is, he's not barking yet. He's laid out on the ground, like he's been asleep. Front paws splayed. His head's alert, ears all pricked and sharp. Soon as Max steps through the hole in the fence, he climbs up.

'Max, watch it,' I say, under my breath – but tonight's so quiet, even a whisper sounds loud. I notice a light come on in the window of the cabin. Shines brown in the small pane of clouded safety glass.

Max sees the dog, waves at me to stay where I am.

And me, I can't watch. Because, yeah, the dog's on a chain, but the way Max is moving, he'll be in range of its teeth any moment now.

Only, see, the dog, it doesn't do anything. It just tips its nose up to smell him, and then Max is there with his hand reaching out, and the nasty mutt that looks like it eats babies for fun, just licks at his fingers.

Honest to God. It *licks* him.

Proper chilled little darling.

And I'm thinking maybe his stage name suits him after all, *The Great Maximo*. Because no doubt this bloke is a magician.

Max, he just smiles at me, and shows me his hand, and I see he's got some chicken nuggets in it. And there's no magic trick, just a crafty mind. He winks. Here we are, I'm thinking, breaking into a junkyard to steal a horse from some hard cases, and he's enjoying himself. I don't have time to catch the mood, because I'm staring at the cabin now, and that small, mean light. And a shadow that's moving behind it.

I'm trying to tell him, Max, but he's still stroking the guard dog's ears, getting real friendly. He doesn't even look at me while I'm waving like an idiot. He moves straight from the dog to the horse. And now he's got his face pressed against the nose of the great white mare. Like he hasn't seen her for years. Like two lovers reunited, which is some happy scene, I get it. But it's going to be a lot less romantic when whoever's in that cabin comes out and finds some stranger in his yard.

Just then, my mobile vibrates. It's Joe, telling me everything's real calm and quiet at the park. *All fine here. Billy dozing. Be safe.*

At least that's something to be glad about.

'*Max*,' I say, still in a whisper, but louder now. And then I've picked up the shears and I start cutting away at what's left of the chickenwire, because there's no way we're going to get that great horse through the gap as it is. Then Max is back with me. He's caught on about the fence, too. And he doesn't bother with shears, he's just climbing up and ripping the wire back from its tacks, pulling with all he's got until the thing collapses.

'The bloke,' I manage to say, while we're going about clearing the way. And I can tell that in all the excitement, Max has forgotten all about the cabin. But now he looks, and when he does, we both see the door of that place begin to open.

'You get her out,' Max says to me. He's breathing hard, face white with heat or emotion or something.

'What are you gonna do?' I manage to say. But Max just heads off towards the cabin, his left hand reaching for the hammer in his waistband as he pushes his way inside. Which makes my heart leap, I can tell you. It's thumping hard, that heart. Swollen. And it doesn't calm down as I make my way to the horse, and begin untying her rope from an iron piling buried in the ground.

I haven't forgotten about the dog, either. But it's got its nose stuck against the dirt now, chewing on the nuggets, happy as can be.

I'm waiting for a bang or something to come from the cabin, because for all I know the yard bloke is armed. But I know I can't hang around, so I get the horse and, very gently, I start leading her to the fence. And she's huge, I can tell you, the horse. I can feel her weight with every step. And not just her weight, but her heat, too. Feels like a furnace next to me, giving off heat. And a smell, like nothing I've smelled before. Pungent and sharp. Like she's made of earth. She sniffs and snorts as I pull the rope, but she comes with me, easy as you like.

I'm not going to lie, though, I'm terrified. My hands all a-jitter, and my thoughts scattered, and not only because Max is in there with the bloke and God knows what's happening. But also because if this animal here decides she doesn't like me, one kick of her hooves would knock my head off.

So I make sure to go through the fence first, away from her back end, pulling the horse after me. She ducks her head, wary of the fencing, but then she's through, and we're both out on the road, the noise of her hooves ringing down the street. Loud enough to wake folk up, I'm thinking. Proper racket.

Then it's the wait for Max. And while I wait I have a quick look at my mobile. No new messages, so everything's calm, I tell myself. But there's no calm in me.

About four minutes pass before Max reappears. He's running my way, and the hammer's nowhere in sight. Then he's taking the rope, a few hushed words to the horse's ear, and we're rushing off in this clatter of hooves that might as well be the sound of my heart thrashing away.

I'll not forget that. Loud, like some jazz drummer doing his stuff. All along the middle of the street, skirting the golf course to get back to the sea front. Down to the quiet bits. To the trail that goes up the coast.

TWENTY-NINE

'**W**HAT DID YOU do to him?'

This is me. We're slowing now, in amongst the blackthorn on a sleepy old bridleway at the edge of the golf course, sea in the distance. The sound of waves just beyond the hedge, like white noise, like the lull before sleep. But I'm not sleepy, not one bit. I'm as awake as can be, and I'm scared. 'Tell me, what you did!'

I don't like violence, and I don't like violent men. Violent men destroy the world, make it impossible to live in. They'd made it impossible for my dad, impossible for me.

'Who?' Max says.

'The yard bloke. What did you do?' My voice is breaking, and my tongue feels thick, like I'm parched.

He doesn't look my way. He's still messing with the horse, slapping her neck, rubbing her nose. He loosens the buckles on the head collar, and adjusts it, reties the rope, making sure she's comfortable. His mind's a long way away, I know that much. He barely knows I'm here.

'Did you – hit him with the hammer?' I ask. 'Did you?'

'He's all right,' Max says, still not looking at me. 'He was an old man. He didn't want a fight. I tied him up, that's all.'

'But you hit him?'

Max's glasses turn to me, and the orange glow from a streetlight at the edge of the bridleway flares in the good lens. He says, 'Hey, I don't hit people, Johnny. I told you, he's not hurt. Don't worry about him. Worry about us, please. Your friends will be after us soon as it's light.' Which is a low blow, and I tell him so.

'Billy's your mate, not mine,' I say.

Max glances at me, this quiet, guarded look. We're both nervy, it's obvious, adrenalin still running through us. 'He was never a friend, not exactly,' he says. 'We drank together sometimes, that's all. Until I found out what he was up to with those fires.'

'How'd you two meet?' I ask. My body won't stop shaking, I'm going like a baby's rattle.

'Billy?' Max shrugs, his hard mouth looks soft, uncertain. 'He was working at the winter circus in Scarborough, last year. That's where I met him.' A pause. The streetlight catches the side of his face, glimmers in the dark of his eye. 'Here, are you all right?' he asks then, looking at me.

I nod, but I'm not. I'm nowhere near all right. And I wish I was home in bed, far from here and safe. His hand on my arm, squeezing, reassuring himself that I'm OK.

We seem to be waiting for something, but I'm not sure what. 'Check your mobile,' he says. 'Johnny?'

I look. There's nothing.

'We'll wait a minute,' he says. 'Calm down a bit, yeah?' While we wait, I look up to the horse, to Half Moon. She's old, but sort of beautiful. The eyes so big and shining.

I ask, 'So what did she do at the circus?' I'm trying to keep my mind off what's going on inside me, because I don't feel well. The nerves have got the best of me. I feel faint.

He looks at Half Moon's wide, placid face, a proper look of love. 'She can do stunt work, tricks.'

I hadn't gone to the circus, never liked them. Dad always had it in for circuses and fairs, zoos, too, because he said nothing should be chained or roped up, nothing alive. Living things needed air and space, he said, and no one has the right to lock it up, especially for entertainment. But Joe had gone to the Christmas show, I remember, and he'd spent all the next day banging on about the trained horses and how they danced like people.

I look at Half Moon's long nose. 'So she's a trick horse then?' I ask, disbelieving, because she looks ancient right now, I think. Older than old Win. God knows what sort of tricks an old nag like this can do.

Max doesn't say anything. He just takes a few steps back, one of his hands held up, close to the horse's eyes. Like he's shielding her from the streetlight. Then he says something, some word I don't recognise. Real quiet.

As he says it, that's when Half Moon starts lowering herself to the ground. Bending her front legs and sort of kneeling down. Never seen anything like it. Steady as you like, she is. Like some lady in waiting at a palace, curtseying before a queen. She waits like that, still as a statue, until Max drops his hand down by his side. And then she's up again, calm as anything.

I don't say anything for a bit. I'd never have guessed a horse like Half Moon could do something so graceful. 'What else can she do?'

'We had this thing where I'd ride her through a ring of fire. Oh, and she swims,' Max says, like it's the most normal thing in the world. 'She's a water horse.'

Fire and water. Proper elemental, she is.

'Horses can't swim, can they?' Only in my dreams, I'm thinking. Horses thrashing about in the sea, the firelight flashing bright in their eyes. But not in real life, not proper swimming.

'Well, Half Moon can,' Max says. 'Back when they had a pool she would carry me around in the water, as good as a dolphin. But the circus is smaller now, less money in it.' He looks at me. 'No pools.'

'Is that why you left?'

I see Max's expression change, lips curl. 'No, I didn't like how they treated her. And they treated me nearly as bad. So I left, and took her with me.'

'You mean, you nicked her?' Finally, I'm catching on. Now I know why Max didn't go straight to the cops when he got out of the hole, why he hid at the park. The bloke's a thief. 'You did, didn't you?'

'Check your phone, will you?' he asks again.

I want to say what's all the bloody interest in my mobile, when I see that I've received something. A video file. 'What's this?' I say.

'It's the proof, Johnny,' he says. 'You're going to have to take it to the cops. I can't do it.'

'Why?'

'I just told you. Half Moon isn't mine. If I go to them, I'll get arrested. It's easy, you just email that file to the coppers or take it into the station, and they'll arrest Billy and all this will be over.'

'You lied to me,' I said, and my voice cracks a bit again, like I want to cry. I can feel the worry in me rising, like something taking away my breath. Poison in my blood. My head starts to ache, to throb. I don't like this. Don't like any of it. 'No,' I tell him. 'You do it.'

'I can't, and you know why. Please, Johnny.'

My chest is tight and there's this big wave of nausea moving through me, thick as lead. My mind is so busy with thoughts I can't settle on one. I'm beginning to panic, so I don't notice the mobile vibrate. It's been buzzing for a few seconds now.

Max looks at me, a bit worried. 'You OK?' he says. 'Johnny?'

I stare at the screen of my mobile. It's Joe calling. I press *Accept* but my mouth's too dry to talk. I'm expecting Joe to say something, but first off it's just a noise that rattles in my ear. I hold the mobile away from me, startled. Max can hear it, too. A voice yelling so loud it's distorting the speaker. When it stops, I put it closer to my ear again.

'I know what you did, you little bastard!' It's Billy's voice, and he's screaming down the phone. *'You and that runt brother. Bring that phone back now or I swear I'll burn the park down, a van at a time.'*

The nausea in me turns to terror. It's as tight as a fist around my heart.

'You hear me, you little shit? Say something.'

If it's never happened to you, you won't believe it. How shock can take you over. Like some bugger's pulled a switch and all your wires get crossed, things won't start, won't work. Like you're a broken toy. And what breaks in me is my voice. Or rather there's suddenly something heavy lying in my chest, making talking impossible. The one thing I need to do and I can't do it.

I see Max reaching out for me, about to take the mobile. He sees the shock in my face. I try to say something, but I can't.

'Say something or I'll torch the whole place and your mam's house with it!'

No, I want to say. *Please*, I want to say. I want to say I'll do whatever he wants, just leave Mam alone. But there's nothing. My voice won't work.

'Talk to me!' And then I hear Billy scream something else at me, and the click of the mobile. And he's gone.

THIRTY

'JOHNNY? WHAT'S HAPPENED? Johnny?'

Max's eyes are wild.

Another wave of that lead runs through me, cold as death. I feel like I'm going to be sick, but when I bend over nothing happens. He's holding me now, trying to keep me on my feet. My body feels like it's tearing, like my insides are twisted up. It's a panic attack, a bad one. I don't know how long it is until I can breathe again, but I think of Joe in his bedroom, and Billy over him. I think of the pain of suffocation, and I wonder how long you can hold your breath until it's too much.

'Johnny.'

For a while it's only the fear I feel. A fear so big it's like pain searing through me hot as fire.

Then something else comes, and when it does the pain goes a little. It's anger. At him, at Max. Because he's the cause of all this.

Dad knew it. He told me often enough, Don't get caught up in another man's trouble. Especially a desperate man. And yet here I am, with a horse that's been haunting my dreams for a week while my home is about to be burned down.

And for what? Some bloke from wherever, because he asked me?

I push him away, and start walking. Back up the bridleway, back to

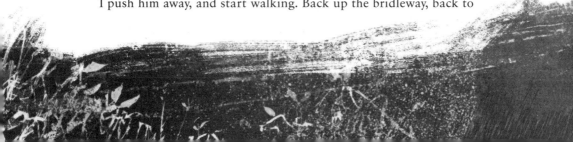

town. While I walk, I call Joe's number, hoping Billy will answer. Hoping I can change his mind. Hoping against hope that I'll be able to speak. But he won't pick up, and so I keep calling. Over and over. And all the while, I'm crying. My body's shaking. I've felt this before, of course. Back then. Back with the Scares and the Shame. Because all this has been for nothing, I tell myself, and it's all my fault. Mam and Joe, back at the park, and Billy will kill them both, and all because I was stupid enough to go to the hole on my own. And where's Dad's pride in me now, I'm wondering? What is he thinking, looking down on all of this?

'Wait—' Max is behind me. Half Moon's hooves slapping against the pavement, loud as you like. I make towards the sea front, along the north cliff. If I run, I can get to the park in an hour maybe. 'Wait!'

Max doesn't know what's happening. Doesn't know right now that Billy's getting ready to burn the park down. And I can't tell him, because even though all I want to do is scream, my lips won't move, my throat won't open. I'm gulping down air, and it takes all my effort just to breathe. Just to keep going.

Another few metres and I feel his hand on my arm, yanking me back.

Bastard, I want to tell him. But I can only stare daggers at him as he looks at my wet face.

'Is it Joe?' he says. 'Tell me what's happened.'

I open my mouth to yell at him, but nothing will come out. And my body folds over now with pain. A panic in my ribs.

'Is it the park? Your mam?'

I manage to nod, that's all. No more than that. And he pulls me by my wrists, straightens me up. 'Your mam? OK,' he says, and he takes a minute, thinking. 'All right,' he says then, and guides me to Half Moon. 'Get on her, climb up,' he says.

And I don't know what he means, but now he's clasped his hands together and he's holding them before me, like a stirrup, and he's nodding for me to step up onto Half Moon's back. 'Come on, let's go.'

I'm thinking he's as barmy as me, because I've never been on a horse. And getting on one isn't like you see in the films. You don't just swing on, one easy move. Not unless you're a bloody pole-vaulter or something. Because she's big, real high. And once I'm standing in Max's hands and he's pushing me up, I still can't get a grip. Her back's dusty, dry. No hold, see. I try to dig in my fingers and haul myself up, but I'm getting nowhere fast. I grab her mane, thinking that will help, but she's moving from hoof to hoof now, wondering what I'm up to, and not happy about it.

Another struggle and I manage to get my right leg across her back. Then it's Max grabbing the rope, folding it this way and that, looping the end through the head collar, making some sort of rein. A minute later, he's climbing on behind me. He groans as he steadies her, and I imagine I hear his cracked ribs grinding again. But he settles himself without any more complaining.

'Just breathe, Johnny,' he says, as he squeezes his calves to make her go. 'I'm going to get you home, I promise.'

THIRTY-ONE

BEING ON A horse isn't comfortable. My legs feel like they're being split apart, and there's nothing for me to hold onto but her mane, which cuts a bit in my palm, leaves the skin sore. Besides, my hands are dirty with her, brown with dust, greasy, so I can't grip too well anyway. It's all I can do not to be thrown off her back as we jolt up and down, but somehow Max holds me steady between his arms, and I grab on as best I can.

For a moment, I wonder if I've gone mad and this is some dream or, better yet, a nightmare. I'm wondering if Half Moon isn't that kelpie from the book of legends come to drag me into the water, into the waves, and drown me. I can just about see the sea in the distance as we make our way into town, so it wouldn't take long if she put her mind to it. Just a glitter of moonlight in the black, and then the slow sinking down under the waves.

I'm dizzy with what's happened; my mind won't settle. I can't take in the streets that we move down, can't focus on the startled faces we pass. Too late for the pubgoers, too early for the shops. Just some of the men and women in the fish sheds on the harbour now, floodlights above the corrugated roofs. Bright against the dark blue sky, fresh now with that early morning glow hugging the horizon. Humming sound of machinery or motors or fridges or something.

And me and Max and Half Moon, just trotting down the road, bold as you like. Half Moon, she stops and smells the fish in the sheds, tosses her head a bit. In alarm or just disgust, I don't know. Then we're heading on, past the dark shopfronts, across the bridge, back to the cliff path, because that's where we're going, like Max says, back the way we came. Back home.

Maybe it *is* a dream, I tell myself. All of this. Because it certainly doesn't seem real. Me and Max on a horse, riding out of town.

We both dismount for the climb up to the cliffpath. And it's a steep climb, all right. Half Moon doesn't seem to notice, though, she just seems happy to be moving, and then we're high up with the sea out before us, me and Max on her back again. There are lights out on the water this morning, on the horizon, these long freight ships that look like islands in the night. Lights on in the pilot cabins so big and clear that, from this distance, you could mistake one for a planet. Only, you notice these planets move, very slowly. Almost too slow to see. Many a time I've wondered about being on one of them freighters, going wherever – Scotland, Holland. Just scarpering. Tonight, more than ever. And if anything's happened to Mam, I will, I tell myself. I'll leave and never come back. I'll run with my Shame and my Sadness and no one from East Ferry will see me again.

Out on the cliff path now, sound of waves beneath us battering the land, like thunder underfoot. Vibrations that run right through your bones. And the rocking of the horse as she picks up pace. Max is urging her on. We're trotting in the border of dirt that tracks the path.

173

'Won't be long,' he says, both his arms around me.

'Nearly there.'

I want to hate him, but I can't. It's not his fault, I know that.
It's mine. I chose to help him, and it'll be me to blame if Mam's hurt.
Or Joe—

The sky's clear. Stars up there, lots of them. Still shining even as the
sky begins to lighten. Then I'm thinking of Sophie, and how much she
made me laugh. We kissed a few times, me and her. And I think about
that, about how warm she was, what she felt like. I'm trying to think
about anything but what lies ahead: Billy's chaos. Because I can't deal
with it, not yet. I can't face it. I'm expecting hellfire and pain. I'm
expecting the whole place gone.

Maybe it's the moonlight on the sea, but right now I keep telling
myself that life shouldn't be like this. It's not what Dad would have
wanted for me. And why not have a laugh and a joke sometime? Why
not fall in love and be happy? Life's short, so get what you can while
you're here, I'm telling myself. And maybe I can find Sophie's number
again. Maybe I'll call her.

Maybe.

Please God, I think. If I get out of this mess, I'll call Sophie and
apologise. I'll set it all right. With Sophie, with Mam, with Joe. I'll get
my life back on track, I promise.

Now the path slides away. Duckboard skitters down. Another chunk
of cliff has gone. Dangerous. Maybe Half Moon senses it, because she
pulls up, starts snorting.

'It's all right, girl. All right,' Max says, but she's not having it, and I don't blame her. The sea churning below, and the bank sloping off. Half Moon isn't daft.

There are fields to our right, beyond the sagging wire fence. Big expanses of grass, safety. Acres and acres of farmland. It's electrified, the fence, but me and Joe have dared each other a dozen times to hold on and wait for the pulse to go through us. Just a pulse, a little charge to ward off the cows, keep them away from the cliff. So, before Max can stop me, I've ducked under his arms, and clambered down to the ground. Then I grab hold of the wire and pull it down under my foot, so Half Moon can cross.

Max understands all right, and soon enough we're in the field and he's pulling me back up. We're in the wide, empty plain of the pasture field. Away from the cliffs, away from the noise of sea. All we have to do is cross a few fields and then we're back at the park. It's a quicker way than the cliff, I tell myself, cuts off a good ten minutes.

But then there's a gleam in the distance. It's inland, so it's not another ship, I know that much. Wrong direction for a lighthouse.

Orange, it is. Bright. General direction of the park, see.

No, not *general*, I realise. It's exactly where the park is.

Orange and bright as flame, bright as fire.

And right then I know what it is. I've been expecting it since we arrived up here. It's my home, and it's burning.

Bloody Billy, I'm thinking.

Bloody Billy. He's done it, all right. He's set the place alight.

THIRTY-TWO

I SHAKE MAX'S arm, to make him see. And whether he does or not,
I'm not sure because we're still trotting when we should be galloping.
Our house is on fire, and here we are having a nice run out. Finally, he
seems to catch on, and Half Moon accelerates, but it's not long until
we hit a stone wall at the edge of the field. Max takes a minute or two
to look for a gate, but there isn't one. And when another minute passes
and we haven't moved on, I wrestle my way beneath his arms, slide off
the horse and start running.

'Johnny!'

I'm not waiting any more, I can't. Not when Mam's in danger.
I need to be there with her, need to save her.

It's not easy running across fields, even with the sky lighter now,
even when the ground is dust-dry. Ruts in the ground churned up by
tractors a month back turned now to crusts as high as your waist in
places. So you fall when you're pelting along, no way around it. But
you don't stay down. You fall-run, stagger-run. Down on all fours,
then up again, spend as much time on your hands and knees as your
feet. And then a scramble over the wall. Another field. More dirt and
ruts and ditches. A fence. On and on it goes. And you don't seem to get
any closer, no matter how fast you go.

Noise of your blood in your head.

Thud of your heart, shaking your whole

body. And that small orange bloom out there, jumping in

the night as you run, never still. Shiver of fire.

And who's dead and who's alive, you're thinking.

Mam? Joe? Win? Where are they? And how many more? How many

times does this have to happen? Your dad gone, and now your mam, too.

This is what goes through your head when you see your home on

fire. The disaster of it all, the pain, charging through your veins like

electricity. And that rabbit brain doing its work, making you run on.

Because you don't feel the burning in your lungs, don't feel the grazes on your hands, or the jagged cut on your knee, bleeding now, caused when you misread the last fence. Your body feels nothing but the urgent need to keep going.

Good old rabbit brain.

Times like this you feel like if it wasn't for that weird brain of yours you'd just collapse and never get up again. Or better yet, dig a hole and bury yourself. Escape from the world. Hide away from its people and keep this agony closed in your ugly heart for ever. The way Dad tried.

So you're nearly there now. Another fence, another field, then the rewilding bank at the top of the park. Then it's down onto the lane – and soon you'll see the disaster of it all. Your loved ones dead and your life destroyed.

That's what I'm thinking anyway. Only, see, it doesn't happen. I'm over the fence and into the wild meadow, when I hear something to my right. Above the rushing noise of the flames leaping from the roof of the nearest van, there's a voice trying to calm others down. Strong voice, and one I've known all my life. I run down the bank, and there she is, silhouetted against the fire.

Mam.

I've rushed into her arms before she's even seen me, but when she does, her face crumples. Tears rolling down her cheeks. 'Oh God, love,' she's saying. 'God.' Just that. She says it a couple more times.

And by rights she should be wailing at me, tearing strips, but she's strong as they come, is Mam. She just holds me tight to her, like she might never let me go again.

I'm all right, I want to say. But I can't speak. I can't even bloody whisper.

She holds me at arm's length before her, confused. She's expecting me to say something, of course. She looks at me all over, searching for injuries. 'You're safe, aren't you? You're not hurt?'

I nod furiously. Then I hug her again.

'What is it?' she says. But she knows. A little bit of her has been waiting for this, dreading the day. She holds my face in her hands – they're hot, her hands – and she kisses my forehead. Then we both jump as something shatters in the van behind us. There's the crash of breaking glass, and then Mam's ushering people away. I recognise most of them, the people around, residents from the park. But there are tourists mixed in, too. A sort of muddled line of them, all looking back in shock at what's happening, faces lit up, waiting for my mam to tell them what to do. And then, over by the front gate now, I can hear sirens wailing. Blue lights flash in the night beyond the roofs.

I follow Mam as she guides the people up the bank, towards the fence, away from the blistering heat. The air's thick with this chemical smell that gets into your lungs, oil and plastic burning, and bits of ash, thin as tattered paper, float about in the air, tar-black. Like a swarm of moths.

I'm looking for Joe in all the mess. Trying to see above the heads of the crowd. The whole park is this riot of noise and movement, and it's dark here, darker than it was in the fields, despite the orange fire everywhere. So much of it, I can't tell how many vans are burning. Three, maybe, that I can see. But more further down towards the square. The fires throw up so many shadows you get lost in them, maze-like.

Strange thing is, I've forgotten all about Max. That is until I see something pale flash in the corner of my eye, skittering through the gap between two vans. Half Moon, I think. I see long legs and her neck cast all jaundiced and yellow in the light of the fire. A streak of her as she jumps a fence, and then she's lost behind the blazing caravans.

So he's come, like he said. Max. This time he was telling the truth.

I've no chance to think about it, though, because now Mam's got her arm around my shoulder, and she's pulling me tight to her. 'Everyone's safe,' she says. 'I think they are, anyway. But we need to get them all to the front gate. Here,' and she's leading me along the fence. 'Take Win on ahead, will you? She's in shock. Keep her clear of the smoke. She got a lungful back there. The firefighters will help.'

And there she is, Joe's gran. Lovely Win. She's still in her shorts and vest, even at this hour, but her face is dark with smoke, like a bad make-up job. I can smell it in her hair, too, on her skin. The fire. She's shaking.

'Hurry, love,' Mam says. 'I'll be with you soon.' And she kisses me, then she's back organising the people at the fence, getting them to follow us.

'Thanks, darling,' Win says, as I take her arm. She looks like she's been crying, or maybe it's the smoke stinging her eyes, because she reeks of it. Must have been close to a fire when it went up. I'm still glancing all about, looking for Joe, because he must be here somewhere. Him and Billy. 'Such a horror show,' she says, sort of sobbing. 'I never thought he'd do something like this,' she tells me. 'God forgive that lad.'

Billy? I want to say. *Me, I hope he rots in hell.*

I want to ask her where Joe is, but my chest is locked shut. Maybe she'd be too lost in her own tragedy to hear me anyway, I don't know. She's pawing at my hand as I help her through the knee-long grass, around the back of the buildings that face the square. As we move to the corner of the first unit, just like that, it's quiet, as though someone's turned off the noise of fires. Flicked a switch. Cool, too, the walls of the shops shielding us from the heat.

'He's evil, Rabbit. Never wanted to think it before, but how can you explain this? And the way he beat Joe—' I feel a pull on my arm, and I have to hold on to keep Win from breaking away from me. 'Oh, Rabbit, he's up by the playground,' she says then, her voice urgent. 'That's where I saw him last.'

Billy? I'm thinking. But no, she's talking about Joe.

'He's hurt. Go to him,' Win says. 'He got away, but if Billy finds him again, he's done for, Rabbit, oh, you've got to get him out of here.'

She's serious, almost startled, like she's waking from a dream. And her hand's pressing against my hand.

'Go get him out of the park,' she tells me, and now she's wrestling her arm away from me, and sort of pushing me. If I didn't know better, I'd guess she was angry at me. 'I'm OK. I can go by myself. You find Joe. Save him.' Another push, and she breaks free, and I look behind, but Mam's nowhere in sight. So I run.

'Go!' Win yells.

I move down the side of the laundry, this short ginnel that leads to the square. More blue lights flash down the concrete, but the fire engines seem to be keeping their distance for some reason. A few firefighters are making their way up the lane, and I see an ambulance park up by the playground. But no sign of Joe.

I cross the square, hide in the lee of the shop, and from here I can see a big fire, flames shooting high into the sky. It's our bungalow, me and Mam's. It's half gutted already, every window blown out, and towers of black smoke spreading up out of the holes in the roof.

He kept his promise, all right. Billy. He torched it.

If Joe was here, he isn't here any more, so I'm about to head back to find Mam, when I notice a commotion on the incline behind the playground. A long, pale head, lean and solid and almost prehistoric. It rears up, a flash of a mane, and then a *thud-thud-thud* of hooves on the ground. There are men there. Four? Five? They're surrounding her, Half Moon. I don't see Max straight off, just the fumble of bodies crushed against the horse's side, trying to hem her in.

Then Billy.

He's there. I see his face, the rage in it burning bright, hot as the fire all around. A spit and snarl of a face. He's wrestling with someone, and I know it must be Max. But he's lost his glasses now, and Billy's dragging him off his feet, onto the ground. Puts the boot in. Once. Twice.

Another kick and Max cries out.

THIRTY-THREE

I'M NOT BRAVE, never have been. Some kids are. You can tell even when they're nippers, when they're no taller than your knee. Some will climb the biggest tree without a thought and others just stand by, watching, timid. Joe's brave, and my dad was. But me, I've always been one to think first, and soon as you start thinking you let nerves creep in.

So it's not because of courage that I decide to do something. It's not because I've suddenly grown a backbone. It's seeing Max take a beating, seeing Half Moon pulled and turned and yanked by her rope. It's feeling that enough is enough, because there's only so much you can watch before you break. And I'm breaking here. What with the fires and Win's desperate face, and the sight of Half Moon's head craning up to the sky as she tries to free herself.

I see Billy pull Max up onto his feet, carting him away towards the cliff, and I make my decision. I start running after them. They've got a head start on me, I'm not even at the edge of the playground and they've already reached the gate that leads down to the beach. Billy rushing Max down before him, and the others forcing Half Moon through, while she rears up.

I lose sight of them for almost a minute as I struggle against the slope, but once I'm leaning across the gate at the top of the cliff, there they are, halfway down the rickety old stairs, heading for the beach. Half Moon's not making it easy for the three blokes as they try to steer her down the bank. But another minute and she'll be down on the sand, too.

I move past the gate, and I'm pelting down the bank, fast. Maybe too fast. I have no idea what I'm going to do when I reach them, either, but I know I need to go. Need to try. It has to end, I tell myself. All this hate has to end.

Like I say, I'm going fast, and it's dark. The orange light of the fires and those flashing beacons of the emergency vehicles don't reach this far, the brow of the cliff keeps it in shadow. There's just the enormous sky with its stars ahead and the blackness of the sea below.

So I don't see what's coming on my right. Don't hear him. Someone moving as fast as me. And then it's all ballistics. Two objects colliding. Force against force. My rabbit brain bristles, wants to fight, but my body has nothing left. And so I'm carried off my feet, and then I'm in the grasses and flowers on the bank. Floundering on my side, the wind knocked right out of me.

Hands on my arms, holding me, and I feel his face against mine.

Joe.

It's him that's pinning me to the ground. And he's talking, saying something, but my ears are ringing. A churning noise going through me, like a rush of water. I don't know what's up or what's down any more.

187

Joe's telling me to breathe. 'Deep breath,' he's saying.

One hand on my chest and one on my face, holding me, gentle.

'Breathe,' he repeats. Then: 'In and out . . . slow—'

I try to fight him off, but his hands go back to my wrists. 'Stay down, or you'll get us both killed. Rabbit, stop!'

Get off, I want to say. *Bloody leave me!* And I'm trying to struggle up, but he won't let me.

'Don't be daft. Leave it.'

I only manage a single, feeble grunt.

'I'm sorry, Rabbit. But I won't let you. Not for him.'

He means Max.

I hate how he's holding me. I want to get up, *need* to get up. There's anger all through me – at Dad, at Max, at Billy. It's burning inside, and it needs to go somewhere. I open my mouth to argue with him, but just odd noises come out, yelps of pain. When he first met me I wouldn't speak, so he knows what's happening, he's not surprised. But I can see the anguish on his face, too. And not just anguish, but real hurt. Damage.

His left eye is swollen shut, lip bust. Win was right, Billy's had a good go at him, I can see that. Looking at his face makes me want to cry, but crying won't do any good now. What we need to do is stop them.

Please, Joe, I try to say.

'No!' He pins me harder, but then something in him shifts, tilts, like this thing that's been hidden from him suddenly comes into view.

188

The picture changes. He stares at how he's grabbing me, and his eyes become wet. A line on his forehead so deep he looks like he's aged ten years. There's a memory inside him, twisting away. He sees himself holding me against the ground, and the desperation in my face, then sees Billy and him in a bedroom. That's what he sees.

Sees agony. Sees torture. Sees evil.

Joe groans, and I'm not sure if he's sick or if he's just tired. But he loosens his grip on my wrists, and he sort of collapses against me, his face on my shoulder.

'God, Rabbit,' he says.

Silence for a bit. I cling onto his T-shirt, feel the heat of his ribs through his back. His heart. Our hearts are beating to the same rhythm. Joe and Rabbit.

'Sorry,' he says. 'Sorry.'

I squeeze him tighter. All of this has to stop, I tell myself.

When it's done and over, things have to change. No more Scares and no more silences with Mam. No more pain for Joe. I need to be better, start over. Grow up. Stop getting myself into these stupid scrapes. Me and Joe, we'll be all right. We'll make something of ourselves.

'East Ferry's full of crazies, Rabbit,' Joe's saying in my ear. A whisper. His voice is broken, scared. 'And I'm one of them,' he says. 'Just as bad as Billy, got his blood in me, haven't I?' He sounds angry, hurt, like he hates himself.

I grab his face and stare at him.

You're nothing like him, I want to say. Because he isn't. Joe's the best. I love him. But I can't say a word, can't make him hear. All I can do is hold him for a bit, until he stops sobbing. Then I roll over and I'm picking him up, and we're both scrabbling to our feet.

Come on, up.

Because it's not over yet. And it won't be until we do something. Whatever happens will happen on the beach in the dark. One way or another, it ends tonight.

THIRTY-FOUR

THE MOONLIGHT FINDS them like toy soldiers planted in the sand, down on the pale band of beach below. Max and Billy. Lit blue, and their shadows cast short. The tideline is a rough chalk line that scuds slowly in, and rumples at their feet, and then is drawn out again as you watch.

Half Moon is still fighting her captors at the base of the cliff steps, kicking up sand and not letting them rest, not for a second. Good girl.

And, of course, there's the steady, calm noise of the waves as the sea swooshes in and out – in and out – that doesn't match the violent scene below us. Doesn't match my heart either, because it's beating like you wouldn't believe.

The tide's out at the moment, but it's hard to tell in which direction it's moving, and I've forgotten the day's tide times. The bay here is small, set within this tight curve of cliff. They're fifty metres tall at the highest points, the cliffs, and falling steeply into boulders and shingle, so it can surprise you here how fast the tide can turn.

'He's crazy,' Joe says, looking down. He wipes his face with the back of a hand, sick of tears now. 'He must be, Rabbit. After what he's done tonight.'

There's different kinds of crazy, I tell myself. My dad was one, I'm another. But Billy? He's something else altogether. Not mad, just bad.

Joe signals for us to move down the cliff. The stairs are no more than worn timber slats barely holding in the bare earth. Real exposed, too. If we try going down that way, won't be long until Billy's mates see us. So, we avoid it. We both slide a bit down the banking instead, hidden by the weeds. The dirt is softer here. It skitters away beneath our heels, and we have to hold onto the thicker stalks to ease our way.

'What's he doing?' Joe asks. 'Why hasn't he scarpered?'

He means Billy. I've been thinking the same. No way he'll get through the park to the road without being spotted, and by now Win must have told Mam what's what, and the coppers will have been called. Soon the roads leading to the park will be clotted with cop cars, ambulances, fire engines – so he's made for the beach, I'm thinking. He's hoping the tide's out, maybe, and a bit of a walk into town, then him and his mates will cadge a ride from someone and hightail it up to Middlesbrough or down to Hull, anywhere they know a pal who can put them up while the drama round here calms down a bit.

But first Billy wants to handle the business with Max.

We're too far up to hear what he's saying but Billy's having words, all right. He shouts something, but it's lost in the wind. Max is on one knee on the beach, his hands held up before him, like in surrender. And Billy railing.

'Leave the bloody horse,' he shouts now, and he strides across the beach, waving at his mates who are still trying to keep Half Moon still. 'Let the nag go!'

I'm so focused on Billy, I haven't noticed what Joe's doing. He's moved further down without me, and now he's clambering through the undergrowth, these plants, sharp as thistle and tall as him. Impossible to hold onto because of the spines, but good cover. I want to tell him to wait, but even if I could speak, I know he wouldn't listen. I've seen him like this before, concentrated, determined.

As I watch I have a bad feeling, this nagging ache at the base of my skull. Deep in my rabbit brain.

Sometimes I hate that brain of mine. Because, despite the fact that it conjures up wolves that aren't there, and gives me the Scares in the night. Despite that, a lot of the time my brain is right. And this is one of those times.

We'll not get off this beach tonight without blood being shed. That's what my brain's telling me.

I can't reach Joe in time to slow him. It's all I can do not to slide down the rest of the cliff on my backside. And down there, Billy's throwing his weight around, telling his thug mates what to do while he leans over Max, ready to finish him.

Joe's not far from them now. But they're not looking, none of them. Billy's eyes are on Max, and the others, they're still reeling away from Half Moon, scared of her. Two have let go, like Billy told them, but the third's holding onto the rope for dear life.

And Half Moon, she's kicking her legs and tossing her head, real unhappy. If she connects with any of them just once, they're in hospital, or worse, and they know it.

By the time I climb down next to Joe, Billy's got Max by the collar and he's dragging him to the edge of the water.

'I hate him,' Joe's saying, beside me. Tears in his eyes. I reach for him, and he flinches, and then blinks at me, and I see his face is full of this yearning. Full of pain and anger and sadness. I can't imagine what he's been through tonight, but it's left its mark and it's not going to fade anytime soon.

Billy's got Max in the sea now, dragging him by his shirt, until he's overcome by the waves that are washing over his head. Until he's choking. 'Think you could grass me up and get away scot-free? Did you, Max?' Billy screams. 'Let's see how good you swim.' Another kick to Max's cracked ribs, and we both hear Max scream.

Horrible, it is.

I can't stand any more, I can't. So before I've got a decent idea of what exactly I'm doing, I'm down on the sand, running across to them. Playing the hero. Playing the fool.

Filled with a madness, just like my dad.

THIRTY-FIVE

I GET AS far as Half Moon before they see me. Billy's mates. One swings for me as I run past, but misses, and already Billy's shouting out to them to leave me.

He drops his hold on Max, and straightens up, watching, as I run over to him. I slide in the sand, losing my balance. It's like one of those old silent movies, because I'm throwing up my hands, my mouth open, but no sound coming out. Making a proper show of myself.

'All right, Rabbit,' Billy says, and he looks me up and down and grins. 'What is it, Rabbit to the rescue, eh? If you've got something to say, say it,' he tells me, this sneer in his voice.

I skid to a halt before him, look down to Max. He's on his back in the tide, doing what he can to keep his head above water.

'Little quiet Rabbit,' Billy's saying, and there's glee in his voice. 'Proper hero, aren't you? If only you had something to say. Well, Rabbit?' he says, leaning down to me. 'Have you got something you want to tell me?'

'He says you're a coward,' Joe yells from the cliff. All eyes turn on him. He's standing up from the marram grass, staring straight at his brother and calling him out for what he is.

'Hey, little brother,' Billy says, his smile vanishing. 'Isn't it about time you showed some respect?'

But Joe's not listening. He's never going to listen to Billy again. 'Enough!' he's shouting. 'No more, you bastard.' And then he starts running down onto the beach. He doesn't get anywhere near Billy, of course, because Billy's mates grab him. And maybe that would be that, normally. Maybe the show would be over, and Joe beaten again, Max drowned, and Billy on the run. But Half Moon isn't finished.

She rears into the air, near pulling the bloke holding her off his feet, then the rope's free. Her hooves struggle for a second on the sand, looks like she might fall, but then three strides and she's already amongst Billy's mates, scattering them in all directions. Two on the floor and the third running for the stairs. Then it's on to Billy.

He stands his ground like a proper hard case, then, as she moves past him, her hooves crashing into the tide, he aims a wild kick at her, missing by a metre. But it gives me enough time to help Max to his feet. And then while Half Moon turns back out of the water, I pull Max further into the waves, away from Billy. We're knee-high in the sea, doing all we can to stay upright, watching it all. Half Moon doing her thing, and Billy raging. He looks like he's going to come for us, so we move further out into the tide, feel the drag of the water at our waists.

'I said I'd do for you,' Billy shouts, looking at me. 'And see if I don't.' When he twists to face us, his jacket falls open and I can see the shape of the knife at his belt. I pull Max deeper into the water with

me, and we fall back, lose our balance. When I look again to the beach, Billy hasn't moved any closer. Something's happened to take his attention.

Joe.

He's yelling at his brother, face contorted in pain, fighting to be free of Billy's mates. He's kicking at them, biting at the hands that hold him. Wild, he is. I've never seen him like this before.

'It's all right, let the runt go,' Billy says, and as soon as they do, Joe's breaking across the sand. He looks like he's going for it – going for his brother, which is a shock, I tell you. Because Billy's always going to have it over Joe, no matter what. Even when Joe's taller and stronger than him, it'll be Joe bending and timid. Bullies. I hate them. Dad hated them, too. Called them Parasites.

And Billy is the biggest Parasite of them all.

I want to yell to stop him, because Joe's right about Billy – he's a killer. I know it in my heart. And Joe might be the bravest person I know, and maybe he can name all the Viking gods, and maybe he can divine water, but me, if I've got a talent, it's to smell death.

And right now, the beach stinks of it.

THIRTY-SIX

J OE TAKES A step forward, no more than that, and, quick as you like, Billy's on top of him, and clouts him hard. So hard, Joe falls to the sand. Billy grins, like he's swatted a fly or something. Like Joe's nothing. And then he turns to us again.

'I'll deal with you last,' he tells me. 'It's that grass I want.' And he points at Max.

It's hard to describe – the night, I mean. Because the sky is fogging over now, the perfect blue-black above has turned grey, turned brown, low cloud flecked with fire. Until now the beach has been protected from the chaos in the park, but the air has grown acrid and heavy around us while we've been down here. Great flags of smoke have slid down onto the beach, and with it, these fire-bright embers that look like cigarettes ends swaying in the air.

And there's no doubt about it – the tide is coming in, pulling me and Max closer, then throwing us apart. A tug of war in the waves. I can hear the sea down the coast crash inland, like some angry giant that's been woken, and now will never sleep again. Proper booming sound.

Thud-thud-thud.

And it really does feel like something punching the ground, something heavy and powerful. Coming in beats, a rhythm to it.

I'm staring so hard at Billy and Joe that I don't see Half Moon alongside us. Because of course, it's her beating in time, her hooves in the water, coming for Max. Her *thud-thud-thudding*, here now, breaking through the shallow tide.

Max, when he sees her, he nearly falls backwards. His face brightens. He reaches for her, arms outstretched. A grimace cutting across his mouth as he hugs her neck, and I see he's in more pain than I'd guessed at. Billy's hurt him bad, but Max can still climb on Half Moon's back, with my help. So that's what I do. I grab hold of his side, handfuls of my dad's shirt in my fists, try to push him across her. The sea churns, Half Moon's wading shoulder-high in it, with Max on her back.

And I'm there, too, so close we might be one, her and me. I'm trying to guide her, because if she's not careful, she'll head straight back to the beach, where Billy's waiting.

So I slap her hide, do all I can to make her turn, follow a parallel line to the tide, carry Max off up the coast, where the beach is wider. Then they'll be free of Billy, because no way he'll be able to clamber over the rocks after her.

We're deep now. The water splashes in my face, gets into my eyes, my nose. A cold shock that makes me gasp. I'm not a bad swimmer, but I've only ever swum in the day, and it's different at night.

The sea at night scares me. You lose your sense of direction. The cold gets into your bones. And my clothes, they're heavy, sodden, my trainers feel like weights. It takes all the strength I've got to lift my feet off the sinking seabed and move forward. Another slap on Half Moon's backside, and she's got the idea, surges through the waves like I want her to, cutting across the tide as it keeps coming in. She's swimming, just like in my dream. But I've not time to wonder at it all before another wave breaks over her, past her, then catches me hard in the chest. I lose my footing, and my head goes under.

Nature is blood and pain and rot, too. Nature is flood and fire. Is all these things. Nature is the shock of the cold against my face, making my skin burn, and the choking salt of the water that fills my mouth. The sting in my eyes. Nature is all these things. And it's death, too. Nothing more at one with nature than death, he'd say. Dad. That was the leveller, all right. No bugger got around that, no matter how rich or powerful. Came to us all, same as to a sparrow as to a man.

Dad saw it.

It came to him, of course. Too early.

Now it's here. With me. Death.

It's been there all along in my sleep. The white horse. Because the horse in my dreams wasn't Half Moon, but something else. Something bigger than a mere horse. Maybe Joe would have known, what with all his myths and legends and stuff. If I'd told him, maybe he'd have explained that the white horse in my dream was death, always had been. Leading me out further, into the waves, into the ocean, until there's no way back. So maybe it was a kelpie I'd dreamed about, after all.

And now here is death and the fire all beating together, surrounding us. It's followed me from my old town, from the woods where my dad died, and it's with me now, under the summer sky. Death in the smoke all around, swirling up into high chimneys, before spinning off to join the constellations above.

I fight the rush of the water, turn and twist, trying to right myself, all the while I'm holding my breath, trying not to swallow any more of it. I'm swept up, then flipped over, dragged back down under the surface again.

For a moment, I think I feel Half Moon's great flank strike me, heavy as a wall. But when I'm brave enough to turn my head and open my eyes, she's twenty metres away in the deep, and swimming like a natural, with Max clinging tight.

I watch a bit longer, until they're safely away, until I can barely see them. Gone and safe. There's a swell that makes my stomach leap. Another wave, and I go under a third time. Then I'm up, and gasping for air, and my hands claw for something to hold onto, and find nothing but the sea that runs through my fingers. The welter. Nothing but hard water and another swell. And my useless mouth opening and closing, and no air.

THIRTY-SEVEN

SOMETHING HAPPENS THEN. It's not my rabbit brain working here. There's no pointless adrenalin rushing through my body, no panic, no desperate urge to escape. What it is, is Dad. He's in me, his courage. Because maybe he wasn't too good at living in the world, maybe he struggled sometimes, but when there was a crisis, he knew what to do.

My head feels clear for the first time in hours. I even feel strong in my body. Strong enough to roll over and find the up and down of it. I sense the scrape of the seabed against the tip of my right trainer, and then I'm planting my heel deep and hard, trying to gain a hold. Another second and my left foot finds some traction, too, and then I'm slowly striding through the oncoming waves. I turn and face the beach, let the next wave, a big one, find me and lift me. I lean back and it carries me forward, back to safety. And I'm looking to the figures on the beach now. To Billy, and to Joe.

Waves crash against my back, and soon I'm stumbling forward into the wash, my knees on the slick, moving sand. The wave drags me back a little as it recedes, but I'm safe again. On my hands and knees on the beach, catching my breath. Safe.

Joe and Billy are still there, but the mates have gone, scarpered. Just them two left.

They look like they've been circling each other, wary. Maybe Billy sees the hate in his brother's eyes for the first time. Patience was never one of his strong suits, and it abandons him now. One swing of his fist and Joe's down again, on his knees.

I see something glitter in Billy's hand. It's the knife. He's bearing down on Joe, and Joe isn't looking. His head's down, face to the sand. He can't see the knife. And all that anger in me, all that fear, it vanishes, just for the moment. My body feels my own again, my chest opens, and I want to scream. More than I've ever wanted. I want to stand up and scream my lungs out. So I open my mouth, and lean my head forward, and yell: 'Joe!'

And don't you know, my bloody voice works. Just like that.

It rings out across the sand, echoes in the chamber of the bay and its cliffs, finds Joe on his knees. So loud, it stops Billy for a second. Just a second. But long enough for Joe to raise his head. He turns in time to see Billy looming, and somehow he struggles up and manages to catch his brother's knife hand.

Then there's almost a pause in the fighting as the two brothers wrestle for the knife. Joe's T-shirt's torn, and Billy's face is bright red, brimming with shock. Because he can't believe what's happening. Joe's holding him still, strength in him he hasn't seen before. Little brother Joe is matching him. And it's like Max says, when you need it, sometimes, you find a strength you never imagined.

And I'm thinking, *Good old Joe!*

Because he never fights back, not with Billy, and now he is.

He's standing up to that bastard
brother of his. After all those
beatings he's taken, all those years
of violence, here he is fighting
back. But then, a second later, that
joy melts away, and I'm thinking
he's going to get himself killed.

'Joe!'

He's throwing himself at Billy now. Both tired, I can see that. Not much of a fight left in either of them. The night has got into their blood, sapping them. Not exactly Ali versus Frazier. Just two blokes scrapping under the dark sky. And maybe you could just pass it off as some brothers' tiff, this, if you didn't know them. But I know Joe.

Joe doesn't fight like this.

Joe doesn't hate like this.

What Joe does is grin and bear it. Joe smiles when he's hurting. Joe takes a beating and says nothing, never squeals, never tells. I've seen him with a bust lip before, and he still won't tell on Billy. No, he charms and cajoles and plays it for laughs. That's Joe.

There's no laughing here, though. And there'll be no happy ending. I remember something my dad said once – there's no more brutal fight than a fight between siblings. He knew two brothers in his regiment, identical twins. And when they fought, he said, they didn't give up. Had to be pulled apart or they'd have killed each other, and then the next day you'd find them sitting beside each other in the mess tent, thick as thieves again.

See, I told you family makes no sense. There's an anger there you don't get with strangers. Blood against blood is the hottest fight.

I can see that here.

Arms flail down, the two of them sliding about like they're standing on ice, can't keep straight. Feet slipping, and then they're holding onto each other, as desperate as drowning men. I can't see the knife any more, can't see who's holding it.

Careful, Joe!

I make my way through the waves, closer. I'm nearly there, just a few more strides away, when I see Billy's fist, and the shine in it. The blade, bright as a shard of ice tilting in the moonlight.

Then they're down on the sand, rolling together. And me, I'm so close.

Just a couple more seconds, that's all. But already I'm too late. I know that. The way they're spinning from each other, climbing back to their feet.

Joe lunges forward. Not hard, because neither have the energy in them. But something breaks in Billy. It's like there's a hinge at his waist, and he just folds over, real quick. Collapses in on himself and falls to his knees. A splash of a wave, another. And I'm still shouting Joe's name, but he isn't hearing. He's staring down at his brother now. Joe's on his feet, and looking down to Billy on the tideline. And I don't need to follow his gaze to see what's happened.

Bloody Billy, I think.

Bloody bastard.

THIRTY-EIGHT

Time folds, too. Folds in on itself, compresses.

I don't even notice when the coppers arrive. Joe's dropped the knife long ago. We've been looking at him. At Billy. He's face down, not moving, but we stare, because there's nothing else to look at now. Just him.

The coppers are here by us, wary at first, trying to work out who's a threat and who isn't. One of them is down there, kneeling on the sand, pumping at Billy's chest, and we know he's dead. You can tell. The way Billy's just lying there. Joe's seen his dead body, after all, like he'd hoped. He's found his treasure, too, but it's not money and gold. It's being free of his brother, and it's priceless for him.

There's lots of talk, and coppers shouting at us. But we can't hear, we're in shock probably, but in the moment it actually feels sort of calm and quiet. Then one of them, he's grabbing our arms, trying to part us, and it's only then I see that me and Joe have been holding hands.

Joe says nothing as he's led away to one side of the beach, while a second copper is asking me something, about my name, where I live. Yelling it at me above the noise of the sea. But my voice is shot again. A pain in my throat, like I can barely swallow any more.

A lump the size of a pebble. He walks with me, leads me away from Joe. There must be about ten metres between us. They put handcuffs on us, and tell us to sit on the sand, that we have to wait, and not to speak, not to move.

I want to tell them it's not his fault, but my voice won't come.

'He had no choice,' I say, finally, but it's no more than a whisper. I repeat it, but the copper nearest me isn't listening, and the rushing noise of the sea against the sand is enough excuse for him not to try.

Another minute passes.

'It was Billy,' I say, my voice cracking and creaking like an old belt. 'It's not his fault,' I say, louder, and now there are tears in my eyes, from the struggle to be heard. 'Billy – he would have killed him.'

The copper tells me to quieten down, looks past me to the cliff, and the ashes that are still tumbling down from the sky, and I'm thinking how it looks like it's the end of the world.

Funny thing is, we're down by the sea but everything stinks of fire, stinks of things burned and gone. My hair's stiff with the salt. I feel old, my skin feels old. I rub my hands against my knees, trying to get the sand off.

I hear Joe's voice then. It rises above the noise of the waves, calm and steady.

'You and me will always be aliens here, Rabbit,' Joe says, looking at me.

I don't register what he's said straight away. My head feels clogged and cold. I look at him, and his eyes are on me. The coppers get agitated, tell us to keep our mouths shut.

'Like that David Bowie bloke,' I say, my voice cracking, and raw. But neither of us laughs. We just look at one another.

'I'm sorry,' he says.

'I love you,' I say.

'Don't be daft,' he says, but he's crying again now. Tears rolling down his face, adding to the sea water and the ashes and the dirt.

THIRTY-NINE

GOD KNOWS HOW long it all takes to get us both up the cliff and into the cop cars. I can't tell when the night ends and the morning begins. None of it makes sense, and afterwards, trying to think back, it's all out of order. My mam arrives, and Win, too, I know that much. This is at the hospital, because that's where they take me. Not the police station, but hospital. Because they're worried I have water in my lungs, think I might have half drowned, they tell me.

I don't say anything, because what is there to say?

After they examine me, Mam sits real close as the coppers ask their questions. Her hand in mine, pressing it to her lap so firmly it's like she's scared I'm just going to slip away if she doesn't hold on tight. I'm still in the same clothes, no shower, because I refuse to change. Every time I move, water squeezes out of my shirt, out of my trainers. So maybe she's right to hold on.

I don't know what to say to the police.

Why were Billy and the others there? Did you see Joe attack Billy?

I just stay silent, because I can't speak, not straight away. The fear in me, holding my mouth shut, keeping my throat dry. And I'm panicking again, because I don't want to be like this. I'm sick of being a rabbit. So I listen to Louise's voice in my head, telling me to breathe, telling me I'm safe.

And I feel the weight on my chest lift. I ask: 'Where's Max?'

'Who's Max?' the copper says, not looking up from his notebook. And I tell him it all, the whole story, and God knows how much he believes and how much he dismisses as a mad lad's talk.

Then it's home, they tell me. But there's no home to go to, any more, so me and Mam end up in a hotel for the night.

The day goes like that, quick as you like.

I sit in the bath, and when I get out, finally, and dry myself, I see Mam's ordered up something to eat, but I'm not hungry. She says do I want to go for a walk, and I nod. 'Anywhere but the beach,' I say. I'm thinking about Happy Sands, of course. But there's no worries there, because the cops have cordoned off the whole of the holiday park. Place is a crime scene. No one's going up there for a while.

So Mam and me make our way through the holiday crowds in town, past the smiling faces, past the amusement arcades and fish and chip stalls, and we stand on the harbour wall, stare out to the sea. We just look at the pale horizon, me and her, and that's when I cry. There, in the noise of everything, the roar of wind and wave, only there can I let it go. Like my moans and my tears will just vanish into the blue, without being heard or seen.

'Is he dead?' I ask, that night, when we're back in the hotel room. I mean Billy.

She doesn't have to answer, just the look on her face tells me.

Billy's dead all right, I know he is. I saw it for myself on the beach – too much blood for him to have made it through.

All she does is nod. And that means Joe's going away for a long time.

'What'll happen to Joe now, then? It's not fair if he gets put away, Mam.' My voice cracks, and I'd be crying now if I wasn't so tired. But I am tired, and sort of numb. She sees as much, takes my hand.

'If they're told the full story, they'll look kindly on him, love. I'm sure they will.'

She knows the whole story now, because I've told her – about the man in the hole, about number forty-six. About how Billy tormented Joe. All of it, no more secrets between us.

'And Max?' I say.

'They'll find him eventually,' she says. 'Unless he can vanish into thin air. It's hard to hide a big white horse for long, isn't it?'

But that night, that's what I dream – Max and the horse, just riding along the beach, and I'm running after them, and just like that they vanish into nothing. Into dust. And I'm alone on the sand, staring around, and the night sky lit up with these small embers, glittering and spinning in the dark. Bright as stars.

FORTY

THE FARM FIRES stopped. That's the thing people remember.

It was the hottest summer on record. Folk recall the days walking the beach, and it was the summer dozens of jellyfish washed up on the sand, all pink and shimmering. In August there was a load of flying ants that appeared in East Ferry, scaring off the tourists for a day. They got in your hair, stuck fast to people's ice creams, but the swallows had a field day before they left. In the rest of the country, people lapped up the sun, got drunk, had parties. But in East Ferry they mostly remembered that summer as the summer of the arsonist.

Mam was right. About Joe. They took pity on him in the end, because of his age and because of Billy's reputation, and I was dead proud of him – how he told his story in court, because he could have hidden it away and toughed it out, like he always did. But he told them everything, no matter how painful. And I had my part to play, too. Just written testimony, telling them what had happened and my role in it, and how, apart from Mam, Joe was the best person I knew, and how I loved him.

Like I said, they took into account all the torment he'd suffered, but he was still banged up in prison. They don't call it that, of course, the courts, I mean. They have fancy names for these places, like youth offenders' institutes and special training centres. But Joe, he calls it kids' prison, and he's not wrong, because two years inside is two years, no matter who runs the place or how much football and table tennis you're allowed to play. And two years right now feels like a lifetime.

No one found Max, or Half Moon. Some say they were both probably drowned, but I don't think so. Not *The Great Maximo*, no way.

For the next two weeks the town was full of coppers and forensics people coming and going. Even the local news got in on the job. TV film crews arrived, pointing their cameras at anyone who would stand still long enough to talk.

Mam kept me out of shot, the best she could, but the attention was all too much for both of us, and without the park job, there was no reason to hang around. Anyway, with Joe gone, the place wasn't the same.

I couldn't visit him for a while, and by then I'd settled back in my old town again, back where we'd come from. We wrote to each other, letters, proper old school, and we talked on the phone, when he could. Him and me.

Joe joked how he got to tick off the things on his list, after all. Yeah, he'd found treasure, because Max's mobile, for a short time, was treasure to him. And when they played the video file in court, there was no doubt what sort of villain Billy was, and how easy it would be to intimidate his brother. Half Moon was treasure, too, of course. And Joe got his name in the papers all right. But it was a bitter joke, he said, because of the dead body, and who it was.

See, how he told it, no one deserved to die, not even a bastard like Billy. He was family, at the end of the day. He asked me to write to Win, because she'd be on her own until he came out, and when he did finally come out, he said, me and him had plans to follow. 'Joe Fludde and Rabbit Hill, remember? You and me against the world,' he said, but I could hear he was smiling as he said it and so I wasn't sure if he meant any of what he said.

He told me how everything in the nick was OK, as long as you kept your head down, and he'd even made a couple of friends. He'd been put in charge of the library book trolley, wheeling old thumbed paperbacks down the corridors and even giving out recommendations to some of the other prisoners, which was ironic, he said, because he had no time for books, just YouTube. Although, he told me he had been reading a few. Comics, mostly. Some weren't half bad, he said. It was like TV if you read it the right way.

At night, he had trouble sleeping, but when he did finally fall asleep, his sleep, he said, was full of dreams. One time, he wrote, he'd dreamed of a party and I was there, and we were dancing together as fireworks went off in the sky above our heads. But as the night went on, the other people on the dancefloor, they turned into horses and ran off, and so did we. Both of us, he wrote, horses running along the sand.

We heard nothing about Max, but when the circus came to East Ferry that autumn, I asked Mam if we could go back to see it. It was odd returning to the coast. We arrived at the circus field, and all I could think about was Max and Half Moon, and maybe I'd see them again. But after a few minutes it was clear there was no horse show scheduled, and so we left.

It was November when a card came. It had been addressed to Happy Sands Caravan Park, and the new management company had sent it on to us. Just a card with a picture of the seaside on it, and on the back, in real small, neat writing was a message: *Heroes exist*. And right off, I knew who it was from.

In the corner of the card Max had drawn a crescent moon, with three stars around it.

My time isn't all taken up with what happened to Max and the horse, though. I still have counselling with Louise – although we do it by video now – and I enjoy walking around the canals and woods, like I used to, and doing chores for Mam. Oh, and I got in touch with Sophie again, which I was proper nervous about. She doesn't live far from where me and Mam live now, so we arranged to meet in the little park in town, and while we walked about under the trees with the leaves turning brown, I told her about what had happened – about the Scares and how they changed me, stopped me from being with her, made me ashamed. Then I told her about life on the coast, about how

I met Joe, and about the trouble we got into. There was a lot, as you can guess, and I wasn't sure she'd be able to take it all in, or even if she wanted to. I wouldn't have blamed her if she hadn't wanted to talk to me at all, given how it ended between us.

But after a few minutes, it felt natural being with her, almost like before. And, as it turned out, she had lots to tell me, too, because it wasn't just my life that had been upended. Hers had, too. Her parents had split, you see, her dad living somewhere down south now with another woman, so it was just Sophie and her mam. But they were happy enough, she told me.

'Oh, and I have a boyfriend,' she said. Just a few months now, but she liked him. Sophie smiled as she told me, like she was really excited about it. But then the smile vanished, and she added, 'Are you all right with me telling you that?'

And maybe there was a bit of disappointment in me. Which is stupid, obviously, because we hadn't seen each other for almost a year, but I said I was. Then I told her how I loved Joe, which felt frightening – telling her, I mean. And I'm not sure if I even used the right words, but she seemed to understand.

'Not that I'll probably even see him for ages, because the place where he's held is miles and miles away. But anyway—'

'You don't choose who you love,' she said. 'And distance doesn't matter. Look at you and me,' she added.

'You and me?'

'We were miles away from each other, but it didn't stop me thinking about you, did it? You still have to make plans,' she said. 'Plans are important.'

I nodded, and felt suddenly embarrassed. When I looked up again, Sophie was staring at me, this expression in her face that I couldn't read.

'It's good to see you again,' she said. 'Really.'

And that day, long after the heat of the summer had faded away and the bloke in the hole felt like a dream, after saying goodbye to Sophie and as I began my way home, I remembered what we'd said back in the early morning light, Joe and me. Silent promises we'd made each other on the cliff, with our hearts beating like drums. And in my head, I started making plans, because, yeah, it will be a long time until Joe's out, but that doesn't mean I can't think about where we're going and what we'll do. How we'll make something of ourselves.

Because my dad always said that promises are meant to be kept, and those made to yourself are ones you must never break . . .

ACKNOWLEDGEMENTS

Thank you to everyone at Andersen Press for the invaluable
support and skill I was given in order to make this book.